Anne J Robertson

Society in a garrison Town

A Novel. Vol. 2

Anne J Robertson

Society in a garrison Town
A Novel. Vol. 2

ISBN/EAN: 9783337046514

Printed in Europe, USA, Canada, Australia, Japan

Cover: Foto ©Andreas Hilbeck / pixelio.de

More available books at **www.hansebooks.com**

SOCIETY IN A GARRISON TOWN.

A NOVEL.

IN THREE VOLUMES.

BY THE AUTHOR OF

"MYSELF AND MY RELATIVES," &c.

"Tyranny is a great evil, and to give despotic power to any individual, is to encourage such an evil."

VOL. II.

London:

T. CAUTLEY NEWBY, PUBLISHER,

30, WELBECK STREET, CAVENDISH SQUARE,

1869.

SOCIETY IN A GARRISON TOWN.

CHAPTER I.

THE PARTING.

THE fact was, that Lucy, with what she considered skilful generalship, had taken the
opportunity of going out of the house, the
moment her mother's back was turned, in
order to hear something of importance which
her lover had intimated (by a little scrap of a
note written in a peculiarly illegible manner,
which he had contrived to send to her during
the day), that he wished to speak to her about
that evening.

Hammersly having been walking up and
down for the last half hour, partly through
Church-street, and partly through the little
street round the corner, with rain and sleet
dropping heavily upon him, was very wet and

very cold, as he waited in expectation of seeing Miss Barr. He was likewise very much
agitated, and so pre-occupied with his troubled
thoughts that he cared nothing for bodily
discomfort. When Lucy, at length, made
her appearance, without bonnet or shawl to
protect her from the inclemency of the
weather, she spoke hurriedly:

"You must say whatever you wish to say
quick," she said, "for I cannot delay a
minute." She did not see how pale her lover
was in the lamplight.

" Well, I am going away on a few days'
furlough," replied Hammersly, after a pause.

" Going away !" exclaimed Lucy, shivering
more than before.

" Yes, I am going to London to see something about my sister."

" I am so glad. Has she written to you at
last ?"

" Well, no; not exactly," replied the
corporal; " but I wrote to her and got no
answer."

" You did not direct the letter plain
enough," said Lucy, who knew by experience how hard it was to read Hammersly's writing.

" Oh, yes, I did, for the letter came back to me with 'not known' written on it; and then I wrote to the person she had been living as governess with, and I got an answer."

Hammersly paused now, and drew a long breath. Lucy thought his manner strange.

" Well, what is the answer ? Did you find out where she was living now ?"

" I am going to find it all out," said the young man, slowly and deliberately. " I am going to find out everything."

" Everything ? I hope your sister is not ill?" said Lucy, who wondered a good deal at her lover's tone and manner.

" I don't know, but I am going to London, and will not be back for some days."

" I hope your sister is well, and that she will be glad to see you, and tell her—but perhaps you may not mention me to her; only if you do, tell her how much I should like to know her—how proud I would be to become acquainted with her."

Hammersly made no reply.

" She may be too high to care about such a person as I am," continued Lucy, who remarked the silence of her lover, and felt a little hurt at it; " and if she is, of course, you need not say anything of me, but it is the truth that I would like nothing better than to be a friend of hers."

Still no reply, while the corporal looked fixedly into the puddles in the street, as they glistened in the flickering light of lamps few and far between.

" Miss Hammersly may be above thinking of a person as inferior as I am, of course," said Lucy, still feeling her pride wounded. " And in that case, perhaps you had better not mention me to her at all. There is no necessity to do so."

And now a dark fear shot across Lucy's mind. Suppose Hammersly was going away from Norham for a longer period than a few days, and had an idea that he might never come back. What if his uncle and his sister should persuade him to give her up, and leave his present state of life for ever ? The rain and sleet came pelting down upon her, but she took no heed of them, though her heart had grown chill with her own surmises, and her teeth chattered almost audibly.

" Will you only be a few days away ?" she asked at length, in a low voice.

"If I am obliged to stay away longer it will not be of my own accord," replied Hammersly.

"Then there is a chance of your being away longer."

"There may be. It is all uncertain."

Again Lucy felt how possible it would be for Miss Hammersly, rich by her own earnings, and accomplished, and associating with gentlefolk, to influence her brother, and persuade him to relinquish the idea of marrying the daughter of a tradesman, when he might look so much higher for a wife in after days. In the space of a few seconds these thoughts came flashing through her mind, and all her pride started up, overcoming, perhaps, her better judgment. She would not ask Hammersly to write to her while away. If he chose to send her a letter of himself, well and good, but she would not be the first to allude to any correspondence.

"I hope you will find your sister well, and spend a pleasant time in London," she said, a little coldly. "And now, good-bye, I must hurry away; and there's the bugle sounding from the barracks."

So hurrying away, with snowflakes lying

like feathers on her head, Miss Barr reached
her own hall-door, which she had left ajar,
for the purpose of getting through it without
noise ; and coming softly into the hall, she
found herself face to face with her mother,
who was standing there with a candle in her
hand.

" Where in the world have you been?
Lucy ?" demanded Mrs. Barr, in surprise.

" Just out for a few minutes, mother."

" What for ?"

" Bidding a friend good-bye."

" At this time of night, and in such a
storm ? What in the world drove your friend,
whoever she is, out at this hour?" and Mrs.
Barr looked very piercingly into her daughter's face.

" My friend is going away to-morrow, and
couldn't see me at any other time," said Lucy.

" Well, I won't be very inquisitive this
time about who your friend is," returned the
mother; " but I must say, Lucy, I don't like
you running out like a servant girl, without
a bonnet, in that undignified manner. I
would much prefer your asking your friend
into the house, and treating your friend with
proper respect."

"I didn't know that mother," said Lucy, with a sigh.

"Well, know it now. Mind, I have not asked you who your friend is; but, of course, I take it for granted she is respectable, and deserving of your regard."

Saying which Mrs. Barr thought it proper to open the hall-door, and, in spite of a great gust of wind loaded with sleet, to look up and down the street, and seeing nothing remarkable, to shut the door again, with a well-sounding bang, and to lock it.

"Father and the boys are out still," observed Lucy, as she saw her mother take the key out of the hall door.

"Well, when they knock we can let them in," said Mrs. Barr, grimly, putting the key in her pocket.

Lucy felt a good deal offended; and yet, if her mother had any unworthy suspicions of her, were they altogether unfounded?

"I can't stand this," she thought; "I must give Hammersly up. I feel so mean and underhand; and, then, perhaps, he not caring very much about me after all, with his sister full of her pride, and—oh, everything is wretched!"

And so feeling very unhappy, indeed, with a strong conviction that her mother was thinking of more things than she chose to mention, Lucy warmed her cold hands, and began to work at her monotonous needle-work, wondering if she gave Hammersly up what other amusement she could find to brighten up even one small part of her dull ife.

"If he gives me up, perhaps it will be all for the best," she thought. "I wish he would, and—I wish he wouldn't.

The next morning, at an early hour, Corporal Hammersly went from Norham on furlough, and any one who had chosen to take particular notice of his appearance upon that day would have observed that he looked more meditative than usual, with a somewhat fixed peculiar expression in his eyes, not suggestive of pleasant thoughts; but I do not think any one who saw him cared much how he looked, for the only person at Norham who was particularly interested in him happened to be very sound asleep when he took his place, by the light of the grey winter morning in the train for London.

The grey morning did not promise a much

brighter noon; the sky was all of one dull, leaden hue, and the sun seemed hidden very far away indeed.

Now and then Hammersly pulled out a letter from his pocket, and read it over, trying to make its meaning out different from what it had seemed to him at first—trying to see if the written words could be altered and turned into others. But no ; the words were there very plain indeed, impossible to be changed. The only hope was that the writer of the words might have written what was not true—might have laboured under some mistake; and to that hope the young man clung as a drowning mortal might cling to some frail thing drifting by like a phantom over a troubled sea.

Looking far back into the past he saw himself as a child at the Priory Farm, playing in the innocence of his heart, and careless of the tyranny of his uncle or his dependence upon him.

" If I had stayed quietly at the farm, and borne everything, it might be better for me now," he thought, gloomy, as the train went hurrying onwards. And then there came more gloomy thoughts still—deadly thoughts

of punishment very terrible—of vengeance
to be wreaked on some one for a great and
bitter wrong.

As the train neared the mighty city, en-
veloped in the vapour of the winter day,
these dark thoughts did not abate one jot in
intensity of purpose. Amid the roar of the
city's hubbub and turmoil, and the rushing
to and fro of human creatures, one fixed idea
possessed Hammersly's mind—an idea which,
excusable as it may have been under the circumstances, was still one that a savage in the
wilds of some uncivilised tract might have
entertained in just such force, and possibly for
the same cause. The corporal's first care on
reaching London was to look for a lodging
suitable to his means, which having quickly
enough procured, he prepared to divest himself of his military clothes and put on others
less remarkable which he had brought with
him, and which had been in his possession
since he first enlisted. However much of a
dandy the young soldier may have been at
other times, he certainly cared little how he
looked upon this day; yet, still his appearance was striking in the costume he had now
adopted. Being equipped in his plain clothes

suit, he left the lodging and took his way through Cheapside and Holborn, where, turning farther northwards, he came to a handsome street, not very fashionable, but where the houses were, nevertheless, large and massive and imposing to look at, and whose owners were, for the most part, people of solid wealth.

Pausing to draw a long breath, Hammersly, whose heart would not have sank at battle cry or sound of war trumpet, grew pale as ashes as he put forth his hand to ring the doorbell of one of these heavy-looking houses. A servant opened the door, solemn-looking as the house itself, not by any means a supercilious menial of foppish aspect, but a grave, respectable man of middle age, who scanned the face of the new comer with quiet scrutiny.

Colouring to the roots of his hair, Hammersly asked if Mr. Kettleby was at home?

"No; Mr. Kettleby hasn't come from his office yet, but he's expected very soon; he generally returns at half-past four," said the servant.

It was very near that hour now, and the grey afternoon was beginning to lose itself in

the darker shade of evening.   Lamps were lit
everywhere abroad.

"I want particularly to speak to Mr.
Kettleby," returned the young man.

"What is your name?"

"It does not signify; I wish to speak about
a person whom Mr. Kettleby knows."

"But I must give your name to Mr.
Kettleby before he sees you.   Excuse me, but
I think I know your face.   You have been
here before?"

Hammersly grew red again, and then very
pale.

"Might I ask if your name is Hammersly?"
asked the servant, lowering his voice as he
pronounced the name.

"Yes," said the young man, after a pause,
and in a low unsteady tone.

The servant now eyed him again with a
mysterious, furtive look, in which scrutiny
was blended with a sort of grave wonder.

"I don't suppose Mr. Kettleby will object
to see you," said the man, who seemed at the
same time a little doubtful on the subject.
"You can walk inside and wait in here till
he comes."

So saying, he led the way to a room off the

hall, simply furnished with a few chairs and
tables, with one or two bookshelves hanging
on the walls, and a window looking into a
dreary little yard.   There was no fire in the
grate, and an old-fashioned time-piece ticked
solemnly on the mantel-piece.   Hammersly
thought it a dreary apartment, not because
it was cold and bare of ornament—for in his
soldier's life he was pretty well accustomed to
desolation and discomfort ; but in the grey
light of the winter evening, and in the silence
which surrounded him when the servant left
him alone, after first seeing, in his grave, quiet
way, that no stray letters or papers were
lying about, some dark thoughts were conjured up in his mind—thoughts connected
with prisons and the dreary existence of con-
victs condemned to life-long penal servitude.
   " And so it has come to this," he thought;
" to this, after all my hopes of being one day
respectable and happy.   There is only one
hope still left—one hope that this is either a
dream or a delusion."
   And then, pulling out that terrible letter,
containing that terrible disclosure, the young
man read it by the fast-fading light for the
tenth time that day.   No need of a brilliant

light to read those words which he knew
already by heart.

The timepiece ticked relentlessly with that
steady measure which seems so often to mock
the flurry and perturbation of human hearts
that beat irregularly. Later and darker it
grew, and then the hall door bell rang, and
then there was a sound of the opening door,
and the fall of footsteps, and the murmur of
voices speaking low; then the door of the
room where Hammersly sat was opened, and
a stout, short, gentleman about sixty, with a
great deal of muffling round his neck, and
more than one overcoat shielding his person
from the cold air, made his appearance.

"You are Thomas Hammersly?" he said,
without vouchsafing any other greeting.

Hammersly replied in the affirmative.

"You received my letter?"

Hammersly said he had received it.

Mr. Kettleby then drew a long breath and
sat down, while his visitor remained standing
with that air of respectful composure habitual
to the well-trained British soldier, though in
truth his self-possession was at present only
assumed.

"Of course you know nothing of your

sister?" said Mr. Kettleby, looking at him steadily.

" Nothing, sir; it is to you I have come for any information about her."

" A very bad business, young man," returned the old gentleman, looking sideways at the corporal, with half-closed eyes, and nodding his head, as he plunged his hands in his pockets. " A very bad business, and might be even worse, if it depended upon anyone but myself."

After thus speaking, Mr. Kettleby looked a long time in the same sideway manner at the young soldier, as if to see how far he felt the effects of his words, but though Hammersly's heart was sinking every instant, he preserved an erect and even dignified bearing.

" You see, Thomas Hammersly, that I do not think of connecting you with your sister, and I am perfectly certain that both you and your uncle, honest James Hammersly, would never look leniently on such a crime as she has been guilty off. I say *crime*, because there is no other name for it," continued Mr. Kettleby, after a pause.

" Then there is no mistake, sir; no doubt of her guilt?" asked the corporal, slowly.

"None in the world. The facts are as
plain as that we are in this room. Not a
mere suspicion—no surmise, but a certainty."

Hammersly almost gasped for breath.

" And so she fled," continued Mr. Kettleby,
while a queer, unmirthful smile illumined his
face for an instant. "She fled, but if I had
chosen to pursue her, young man, and employed the police, and done as others would,
she would now be safe enough out of harm's
way; but I didn't, because in the first place
doing so would not have made things any
better as far as *I* was concerned, and in the
next it would have taken an immense deal of
time and given me an immense deal of trouble
to do it, besides bringing disgrace on honest
James Hammersly, her uncle.

" What I have lost I have lost," he said,
nodding his head again at Hammersly, whose
figure was becoming rather indistinct in the
gathering gloom of nightfall; " and I don't
wish to lose more. I'll never try to punish
Rachel Hammersly, and I only hope she
may never fall into worse hands than mine.
Depend upon it, young man, your sister will
not reform all at once. Such a step as she
has taken will not be the last of the kind;

but I will leave it to others to make an example of her for the public safety. If I thought it likely that there were many such young women in the world I might have been led to punish her myself; but as it is I don't believe there is another such being in England at the present moment."

" You mentioned, sir, that you thought somebody else had induced my sister to act as she has done," said Hammersly, in a low, agitated voice, as he tried to gulp down a rush of indignant feeling that made him quiver.

" Yes, I mentioned that; and I think so still. My wife considered that your sister was not altogether going on satisfactorily for the past year, neglecting her pupils, and otherwise conducting herself in a manner very unbefitting her calling. With anything, however, but the one great crime she has been guilty of, I have nothing to do particularly. She may have had an accomplice, or she may not. My servants consider it probable she had."

To the servants Hammersly thought he should now apply for further information on the subject ; and, as it had by this time grown so dark that Mr. Kettleby's stout

figure began to look like a shapeless mass,
and the furniture of the cheerless room to
fade into indistinctness, he considered it right
to terminate his interview with the master of
the house.

"I pity you very much, Thomas Hammersly," said the old gentleman—intending,
perhaps, as much to convince the young man
of the pitiable state he should feel himself
reduced to as to express any feeling of com-
passion for him—"I pity you extremely;
but I do not identify you at all with your
sister, and, if you will remain and take some
dinner, you shall have it with welcome."

"No, thank you, sir," said the young man;
"I cannot remain any longer. I must try
to discover something about this dreadful
mystery. Anyone who knew the principles
of my sister must feel astonished—"

"I know nothing of anybody's principles,"
interrupted Mr. Kettleby. "I go by facts—
by deeds—by certainties."

"Of course, sir; but it is my duty to search
into causes—to endeavour to penetrate the
mystery as far as I can," replied the corporal.
"Good evening, sir, and thank you for your
kindness and forbearance."

Saying which the young man advanced to the door, and went forth once more to the hall, where he found the grave servant man standing in very close proximity to the door he had just issued from.

" You remember Rachel Hammersly ?" said the corporal, in a hurried, almost inaudible tone, as he addressed the servant.

" Yes ; it isn't many weeks since she was here."

" And you knew of a person—a young man—she used latterly to be acquainted with ?"

" Yes; we all knew she had taken up with some youngster. I've seen him a few times myself, and the pantry boy saw him, and the nurse often came upon them walking together in the square and in other places."

" What was his name ?"

" We didn't know."

" Was he a gentleman?"

" It is hard to say. To judge from appearance he might have been anything ever so high, for his dress was good, and his look altogether was grand enough ; but you see as to being a real born gentleman, with the principles of one, it ain't so certain that he was much of that."

" Would you know him if you saw him ?"

" Well, I might, and I might not," said the man, who began to think probably it would not be pleasant to be mixed up in a disagreeable business of identification, and so forth. " It's hard to say whether I mightn't take some one else for him—they're all so like."

Who the " they " might be who were so much alike was left for Hammersly's own sense to determine.

At this juncture a youthful figure adorned with many buttons made its apparition in the hall, and lighted the lamp hanging from the ceiling; after which feat he gazed with infinite curiosity at the corporal, who was now revealed to his sight with considerable clearness.

" He's her brother," he said to himself, with a wicked leer in his youthful eyes; " and precious like her, too. We had better have an eye to the silver spoons, I expect."

And then, vanishing into the obscurity beyond the lamp-light, he listened with outstretched neck to whatever more might be

said by Hammersly and the elderly servant.
But that highly-respectable individual did not
consider it prudent to enter into any very particular explanations touching the young man
whom Rachel Hammersly had chosen to keep
company with; knowing, as he did, how
likely it was that a hot-headed youth like
Hammersly might get himself and others
into trouble for no useful purpose. So he
began to give vague answers to the corporal's
minute inquiries, which were most unsatisfactory; and at length the young man was
leaving the house, very little, if at all, wiser
than when he entered it. When the door
was about to close upon him, the youthful
figure adorned with buttons, and whose eyes
still gleamed with intensely-wicked feelings,
flitted out after him, and whispered in his
ear—

"I know the person your sister used to
walk with, and he has just passed on the other
side of the street. There he is, knocking at
that house, close to the lamp-post—No. 10.
He is very often there. A regular swell,
ain't he ?"

And with this information—imparted altogether through a spirit of mischief, though it

was quite correct—the young tiger, or pantry boy, or whatever he may have been named in the Kettleby establishment, ran back to the house, leaving Hammersly to follow his own devices with reference to the object of his most deadly vengeance.

CHAPTER II.

SETTING OUT FOR HALESBY.

WHEN Ellinor Bouverie received Lady
Halesby's note asking her to spend some time
with her, she felt that she should like to accept
the invitation, and, for a few minutes after reading the missive, a bright gleam of sunshine
seemed to glance across her mind, which the
reader may remember was filled with dreary
troubles at the time the note arrived.

" Will you go to Halesby ?" asked Dora.

" Yes, if I can."

" I think you ought. I should like to go,
too, if I were asked. I should be glad to get
away anywhere out of this dismal house. If
I were a man, how quickly I should be off to
push my fortune, as our old nurse used to say,
and bid good-bye to home, and dependence,
and poverty for ever !"

And speaking thus, not at all in jest either,

Dora Bouverie, with her lips rather firmly set,
and her eyes still beaming brightly, stood
looking out of the window upon the dark pros·
pect without, thinking, probably, what she
could do as a woman towards gaining money
and independence, and a way of escape from
her dreary home.   Leaving her to her reflections, Ellinor went to consult with her mother
respecting this visit to Halesby.   The first
question concerning the matter referred to
money.   Miss Bouverie could not ⸢go to Lord
Halesby's without a little expense, and, although twenty years of age, she had not a
shilling she could call her own, nor the prospect of having such.   Were she thirty—ay,
forty—her position would be no better in that
respect, as long as she remained a single
woman under her father's roof.   No doubt
Captain Bouverie thought it hard enough to
feed and barely clothe his wife and daughters,
without providing the latter with pocket-
money.   He had always given his son
pocket-money from the time he was ten years
old till he was seventeen, because other men
gave their sons pocket-money, and he had a
respect for Dawson, because he belonged to the
sex that is privileged to work honourably and

gain money; and probably he thought he might be a credit to him yet, though in what way was not very clear. Whereas he had always looked upon his female children as inflictions of an unfortunate description. Where the laws and the government of a country are unjust towards one sex, individuals will naturally become so likewise. Scarcely one man in ten thousand is capable of thinking originally, or forming an opinion of his own; the great mass of people are but too prone to mistake artificial distinctions for the work of nature itself, and the laws having decided that women are inferior to men, it follows, of course, that the great body of men take it for granted that there is good reason for such decision. Few men take a sufficient interest in the matter to inquire into it particularly, and women, whom the question so vitally concerns, are not represented at all in the Legislature of the county. How energetically members of Parliament will crowd to pass a bill respecting hares, pheasants, and partridges, what excitement will prevail among them on the interesting subject of game! But when a question concerning the advantage of women alone is to be discussed there is often a diffi-

culty to form a house at all—so lightly does
the welfare of the female (and larger) portion
of the population of this country affect the
senators of Great Britain and Ireland.

Generally speaking, the provision of young
women is looked upon as a sort of joke—a
thing to be lightly regarded, and as depend-
ing in a great measure upon chance. There
is no settled manner of going about the
business—it relies for success chiefly upon
the caprice and the passions of men. The
gambler who seeks to gain a livelihood by
winnings at the gaming table is pretty much
in the same condition as the portionless
young gentle-woman who is going out to
parties night after night, " taking her
chance " of captivating some man who
will in future provide for her, but never ac-
knowledging openly what she is really looking out for. Such candour would be shocking.
In fact, it is quite a reproach even for parents
to be suspected of having an eye to the provision of daughters; and what must it be for
the charming daughters themselves to be ac-
cused of such monstrosity ? Until gentlewomen can have a position of their own, and
a way of acquiring money by professions of

their own, independent of men and marriage, great numbers of them will be forced into marrying who would much prefer a single life.

However Captain Bouverie might despise women in general, and his wife in particular, he was very glad to get the money her aunt, Mrs. Tredcroft, bequeathed to her, and to make use of it for his own and his son's benefit. It was invested in securities in his name, and he it was, of course, who received the interest of it half-yearly.

Poor Mrs. Bouverie never saw nor knew how the interest was paid, nor knew what happened to the principal; she scarcely felt herself the richer by a shilling since the bequest fell to her. Her husband doled out money to her for the house-keeping just as stingily as before, and took all the authority and all the rights that the law of England permitted to him.

Mrs. Bouverie was a miserable woman, but no one knew, save herself, how miserable. Married against her will, she had never been interested to a great extent even in her children, but, like thousands of women, she kept her thoughts and her miseries to herself. If women were not afraid and ashamed to speak

of their wrongs and sufferings, what fearful
revelations, what a mighty outburst would
re-echo through the world! The wretched,
oppressed creatures, who try to go forth into
society, and to keep up appearances for fear of
bringing down the contempt and wonder of
that society upon them; whose worn and
hollow cheeks and altered aspect within a few
years after marriage alone tell of unhappiness
and broken hearts, could reveal in words
many a tale of tyranny and cruelty that
might make men blush, if women were not
cunningly taught to believe that the less a
woman makes her feelings and her wrongs
public so much the more refined and womanly
she will be considered—that is, she will not
be thought of at all. She will preserve her
proper character of nullity, and sink into her
grave in the same obscurity that she has
passed her life in; while the world will go on
thinking that women are very contented,
very well cared for by the laws, and that it is
only a few absurd, "strong-minded," unfemi-
nine, unnatural women, who set up their horn
and complain of wrongs and injustice, and
the want of a reform in the existing state of
affairs.

It is a great fact, however, that women, as
a body, are far from being either happy or
contented. Not alone is it the few literary
women that write openly of these matters,
who understand and feel the oppression and
the bondage that crush the energies of their sex
and humiliate them; it is the great mass of
women in every rank or class of life—the un-
lettered and the learned, the poor and the
rich, the lowly in spirit, and the proud of
heart. She who feels this oppression most of
all is the quiet, deep-feeling, sensitive woman
who is too generous to seize the reins of
tyranny herself, and to carry warfare into the
enemy's camp without waiting to be trampled
on in the first instance. She who feels the
oppression least of all is the unreasonable
woman who becomes the oppressor herself,
who laughs privately at laws, but would not
have them altered, because she likes the idea
of other women being kept down by them.
Heaven help the man who is married to the
woman given to lecturing other women on
the duties of unlimited obedience and meek-
ness.

Having consulted with her mother respecting the visit to Halesby, Ellinor found, to

her surprise and satisfaction, that Mrs. Bouverie could spare her the little money she
required to enable her to accept Lady Halesby's invitation, and a bright gleam of sunshine seemed to light up her mind, as she
wrote her answer to her kinswoman.

The carriage belonging to Lord Halesby,
which it may be remembered Mrs. Barr had
told Mr. Trydell she had seen standing at
the gate of Evergreen on one particular
afternoon, had been dispatched thither by
Lady Halesby to convey Miss Bouverie to
the park; and the latter, having arranged
everything at home as satisfactorily as she
could, and obtained a promise from her sister
that she would take care of the housekeeping
during her absence, which might not last above
two or three days, Ellinor at length took her
place in the ponderous vehicle, with a small
carpet-bag, and a box of goodly size stored
somewhere out of view.   Captain Bouverie
had scarcely been consulted at all about the
visit, as it was not considered necessary, further than to let him know where his daughter was going to.   Her mother's evident carelessness on the subject was enough to ensure
her father's approval of her accepting an in-

vitation to Halesby; while Ellinor was prudent enough not to display any of the pleasure
she felt in doing so; for even she, alas! was
fully aware of the contradictory nature of her
father's temper.

When she had fairly got into the carriage, and found herself moving at length
from the gate of the Villa, she tried to forget
past annoyances and to look forward to a
few days of freedom from household troubles.
Who is there that cannot understand the
happiness of getting respite, however short,
from dreary hours of business and worrying
cares? Ellinor had suffered a great deal of
late, and even still there was a heavy weight
of undefined foreboding pressing on her mind.
What the future might bring forth she scarcely
dared to think steadily upon. For the present
she would try to be happy—try to remember
nothing but that she was going to enjoy a
pleasant visit to people she particularly
liked.

The carriage rolled on to Norham without
interruption; but on arriving at the town it
stopped, to permit Ellinor to get a few trifles
she required at one of the shops. She did
not alight, however; and while waiting at

the shop door, Mrs. Dart espied her as she
passed along the street; and having ascertained that she was the only occupant of the
carriage, the old lady, with a smile, not exactly of pleasure, on her face—but one of
wonder, mixed with a *soupçon* of amusement
and envy—hurried over to speak to her.

"My dear, I had no idea it was you, sitting up so grand in the carriage," she said,
looking sharply to examine the texture and
material of the lining and cushion covers of
the vehicle. " I thought it was at least some
great person—some one going down, perhaps,
to Halesby. But how does it come that you
are all alone in it?"

"I am going to Halesby," said Ellinor, who
felt almost afraid to reveal the fact, so greatly
did she stand in awe of Mrs. Dart's malignity.

"Down to Halesby! That's something. And
they sent the carriage all the way for you? or
very likely they had to send in for something
to town, and thought they would save you
the expense of a fly. I hear Lady Halesby
is very considerate that way to people of
small means. She isn't a bit proud with her
inferiors."

"She is a most excellent woman in every way," said Ellinor.

"Very eccentric I hear—very," continued Mrs. Dart, lowering her voice for fear the footman might hear her, as he stood on the pavement. "In fact, some people think she is not altogether right in the upper storey— makes too little of herself going among the poor, for one of her rank. I suppose it is she who asked you to Halesby?"

"Yes; I should not have gone on any other invitation," said Ellinor, colouring; and she was about to say something in defence of Lady Halesby's rationality, when she stopped herself, feeling that the case required no interference on her part.

"And how long do you stay?"

"Some days, I believe."

"So long! Well, that is very odd. And none of the family asked but you? So queer. You will feel very awkward in that great large house, with such state, after your own home and your one maid. Ha! ha! You are quite like the lady in the lobster, I declare. People will say you are wanting to show off if you stop at any more shops buying things, they are so full of ill-nature and

c 5

gossip.   By-the-bye, is Dora really to marry
the Barrack-master Clarke?   People are
talking of it, I can tell you, and I scouted the
idea, for you know he is a low kind of person.
I don't think Lady Halesby would like that
kind of connection; so if there's anything in
the report, I would recommend you not to
entertain much hope of captivating young
Lyon. Ha! ha!"

Ellinor grew very pale, and turned positively sick at heart, she knew not why;
but there was something in Mrs. Dart's
maliciousness that made her feel quite downcast. That was just what her kind relative
desired. It was too bad to see a young girl
like Ellinor " cocked up" (as she termed it)
in a nobleman's carriage, going on a visit to
the nobleman's house; and she would not
suffer such conceit and pride to exist without
an attempt to take both down.

" I lay you the mother wouldn't have asked
you to Halesby if she had an idea that young
Lyon cared about you or Dora; and mothers
generally know who their sons admire, so you
may be sure he hasn't a notion of either of
you. That's a disappointing kind of thing
now, for I had hoped he would take a fancy

to one of you. Stranger things have occurred."

Miss Bouverie could not keep back the flush that mounted to her cheek, but she was too well accustomed to Mrs. Dart's malignity, which at times verged on gross vulgarity, to permit herself to give way to any indignant speech.

" If I had gone to see Mrs. Dart and Mrs. Sharpoint and told them of this visit yester-day, I should not have been tormented now," she thought, as she leaned back in the carriage somewhat out of spirits.

A spiteful tongue, even though it may belong to a person for whom we entertain little respect, has power to wound often very bit-terly. The very fact of having excited envy and malice was painful to Ellinor. She was not like some people who enjoy making their acquaintances jealous, and look upon such a feat as one of the pleasures belonging to success and good fortune.

" I expect to find Miss Nelly quite set up above herself by this invitation," thought Mrs. Dart, as she retired ignominiously out of the way of the horses, which had now begun to grow restive. " But what

a tremendous thing it would be if young
Lyon really did care for her! It would go
near turning her head, with no fortune and
only one servant, and nothing but pride to
keep the Bouveries so high as they are. I
don't think it would be for her good to be
raised to such wealth and rank; I don't, indeed. She ought to refuse him if he asked
her. But there is no chance of his doing so.
He isn't a fool, and she is not such a pretty
girl, and she's not so young either. When I
was twenty I thought I was quite *passée*, and
she looks very pale and faded to-day—very.
She will alter very soon in looks, and what is
a woman without looks?"

If poor Mrs. Dart had considered herself
passée at twenty, she must have made up her
mind never to have been " present " for the
last forty-five years. A foolish mortal, no
doubt she was; but let the " superior sex "
show their indifference to such vanity and frivolity as the over-appreciation of female beauty
and as they possess the lion's portion of the
money and influence in the world, the other
sex will soon follow their example. Women
know very well what is for their own advantage, and by what means they can make

the most profit ; and, perhaps, if we reflect a
little, we will find that their present regard for
their personal appearance and its adornment
should not be termed vanity, but rather substantial worldly wisdom. Beauty often gains
them honour and wealth, and raises them up to a
high position. Becoming and fashionable dress
enhances beauty. The poor dowdy girl, let
her be ever so pretty, cuts but a sorry figure
among smart young women; and though a
few rare men may admire her, yet, on a
general principle, she will find herself neglected for her better-dressed companions.
Therefore, though a love of dress, and a wish
to be beautiful, may be worldly feelings, they
are neither foolish nor vain, as far as concerns
her temporal interests, for a woman to indulge
in before she is settled in life. Men are not
consistent when they turn round and sneer at
women for taking an absorbing interest in
their personal attractions, which, under the
present system of things, so materially promote their temporal advantage. They may
be certain that the generality of women would
be very happy if it were discovered that they
had no serious reason to trouble their heads
about the amount of their years, or the fleet-

ing character of their youthful beauty. Not
on women let the blame of frivolity rest—not
to their charge be it laid; for what seems to
be frivolity on their part is often but a weari-
some toil and a torment to themselves, carried
on for very important, business-like purposes,
with much care and vexation of spirit.

CHAPTER III.

THE ARRIVAL AT HALESBY.

IN the advancing gloom of the winter afternoon, which was now verging towards evening,
Ellinor found herself stopping at the entrance
to Halesby which opened on the Norham
road—a fine old gateway, with an antique
gate-lodge, and a forest of dark ivy hanging
over the massive grey stone pillars. The
large gate being locked, it took some moments
to have it opened by the gatekeeper, a woman
of shrewd expression of face, highly respectable and trustworthy, whom the reader may
possibly recognise as that excellent person,
Mrs. M'Stare, who some time ago proved herself so much averse to the intrusion of strol-
lers on her master's premises. Respectful, but
not by any means obsequious in her demean-
our, she dropped a slight curtsey as Miss
Bouverie's hat appeared at the window of

the carriage, and though the young lady
smiled and nodded, the woman never relaxed
a muscle of her face. Not that she had any
particular dislike or objection to Miss
Bouverie, but smiles were not easily conjured
up to Dame M'Stare's visage, and she was
not a person who would give herself any
trouble without getting payment in money for
it. Ellinor looked out at the picturesque
gate lodge, which in early childhood had been
an object of admiration for her, and she seldom passed it even in later years without
giving a glance at its quaint roof and Gothic
windows. Driving quickly by it now she did
not see the picturesque face, pale as a marble
statue, and scarcely more animated looking,
that appeared at one of the lodge windows,
looking at the carriage passing by. Probably
the owner of that pale face saw the girlish
countenance and girlish smile of the young
lady who looked out of the carriage
window to greet Mrs. M'Stare; and though
Ellinor Bouverie had very little colour in her
cheeks, and often a sad expression in her eyes,
she could give a very bright smile, which was
all the more charming for the sudden light it
seemed to cast over her pensive features.

There was no look of haggard care, or self-reproach, or remorse, expressed in her face. Whatever reason she had to look sad and thoughtful, consciousness of wrong-doing on her own part had nothing to do with it. In this she presented a great contrast to that of the young woman watching her from the interior of the gate-lodge. The one face, so serene, so exalted, one might almost say, in its shadowy thoughtfulness; the other so wild, so marked with the lines of care, and the traces of some great mental struggle. A bitter face that last was; unpleasant to look at, in spite of its extreme beauty of feature—perhaps all the more unpleasant for that beauty of feature, coupled, as it was, with so much that was unlovely in expression.

Halesby was an ancient house, solemn, and grand, and sombre; but Ellinor thought it the most charming of houses. In childhood she had loved above all things to go to this grey old mansion and dream romantic dreams there, and people it with beings of her imagination, and fancy this room or that room was haunted; and yet among all the wild creations of her child's active brain, she never pictured to herself one half so startling as

the reality that was coming for her connected
with that ancient dwelling—a frightful reality,
coming very soon, too; every passing hour,
every minute, bringing it nearer and nearer.
And she so unconscious of it all.

The carriage stopped at the entrance; and
getting out of it quickly, she ran up the steps,
and into the large, lofty hall, which, amongst
other traces of the past, retained the old-
fashioned cramps, for the great piles of wood,
which, in olden times, our ancestors loved to
have blazing on their hearths; there was also
a handsome marble chimney-piece, supported
by massive figures, and various trophies and
strange old weapons of war adorning the
walls. Ellinor knew everything about the
place too well to pause to examine anything,
even if she had been able to see distinctly in
the gathering gloom, and, following a servant,
she went on to the room where Lady Halesby
generally sat—a warm, rather small apartment—furnished comfortably, but not remarkable for the richness of the adornings.

Lady Halesby was a woman past fifty, of
the middle height, with a figure still remarkable for its extreme elegance—a fragile-looking
figure, very delicate in its proportions. She

wore no cap, and her hair, which, as yet,
possessed no lines of silver to mar its dark
colour, was arranged simply, but in such a
way as rather displayed than disguised the
beauty of her head. She was dressed in a
plain black gown of some woollen material, a
jet chain and jet bracelets being her only
ornaments.

Of an old, distinguished family, Lady
Halesby was remarkable in youth for beauty
and a brilliant career—brilliant at least for a
woman. Courted, flattered, rich, and possessing numerous suitors for her hand, she had
not married very early in life, and when she
did marry people said it was not for love. Be
this as it may, she made an excellent wife,
and for some years past had given up all the
gaieties and frivolities of fashionable life.
People hinted that she had some mysterious
matter preying on her conscience, and that
she was endeavouring to make amends for
past errors by leading the life of an ascetic
now.

Very handsome still, but of a severe style
of beauty, with eyes that expressed no changes
of feeling, and presented a somewhat stony
aspect at all times, Lady Halesby looked

extremely distinguished, and what is called, aristocratic, though in truth the look does not always belong to the highborn.

She went forward to meet Ellinor with much kindness and good-feeling expressed in her manner. She kissed her on the cheek, and thanked her for coming; but, like her gatekeeper, Mrs. M'Stare, she was a woman that never smiled. A man, and a woman too may smile a great deal, and not be any the better at heart for it; but still a sweet smile is pleasant to look at, and no one admired Ellinor Bouverie's beautiful, sunshiny smile, more than Lady Halesby herself.

" You know, I suppose, that I take a great interest in you all at Evergreen," she said, as they sat in the cosy little sitting-room, by the light of the fire. " I think your mother deserves a great deal of credit for the way she has brought you up ; and from what your father says of Dawson, I look forward to his being very distinguished some of these days. There is a great deal in a young man having good principles as well as talent. In fact, I think honour and uprightness of character are more likely to get people on, even in this world, than more brilliant qualities."

"Oh, Dawson has very high principles,"
said Ellinor, confidently. "I am certain he
would never stoop to anything mean." She
did not add that she feared her brother was
careless, and thoughtless, and rather selfish.

"I am sure of that, because all his family
had good principles. I think Lord Halesby
has a stricter sense of honour and justice than
any one I ever saw; but he sometimes
strikes me as being too severe towards those
people who fall short of his own high standard. We should not forget to make allowances for different dispositions and different
circumstances. All people cannot be judged
alike, Ellinor. To whom much is given,
much will be required, and that saying ap-
plies to mental gifts as well as to others. The
clever man or woman who makes an evil use
of talent and genius will have much to answer for on the last Great Day. Those also
who have enjoyed wealth and prosperity in
this world, and who have failed in their duty
to their poorer brothers and sisters, will have
a sad account to render to their judge," continued Lady Halesby, as she looked with fixed
eyes into the fire. "Ellinor, I hear you are

very good and charitable at Norham, and go
about among the poor."

"How did you hear it?" asked Ellinor,
blushing, yet smiling too.   She was gratified
that any one should have taken the trouble to
mention her humble acts to a person so far
from Norham as Lady Halesby lived.

"Ah! people mention those things very
often.   They come round by accident.   The
poor are very grateful for any kindness.   I
have a great many poor *proteges*, old and
young, and I am building a few cottages near
Halesby for reduced persons of respectability.
They are nearly finished and very pretty.
You must come and see them.   Gerard told
me to-day they were putting the paper on the
walls.   I intend them for old ladies who from
any cause except their own ill-doing are left
in want, and each of them is to have an
annual sum of money—not very much, for I
have not very much to give, but still enough
to support them in some degree of comfort.   I
think few people are aware how badly off
several women of respectablility are in their
latter years.   Widows and single women are
often in a shameful state of destitution, and

people seem to take it for granted that it is a
natural consequence of their position. I have
heard such dreadful accounts of the misery
of poverty since I have begun to take an interest in such matters! Do you think, my
dear, that if you had a large property, and
were by any means to become the mistress
of a great fortune, you would preserve
your present simplicity of manner, and
not grow worldly and vain?" And as she
spoke Lady Halesby fixed her stony, expressionless eyes on Ellinor's face, and took her
small hand in her own.

Ellinor laughed and shook her head.

"I am afraid to answer that question,
though I might safely do so, by placing myself in a most amiable and exalted light, if it
were not for conscience-sake, as it is very
unlikely I shall ever be tempted with the
possession of the large property, Lady
Halesby. But really and truly I could not
say what effect great prosperity might have
upon me. I only know that I never expect
any particular good fortune to befal me."

"And you are quite contented with your
present lot?"

Ellinor did not answer that question very
quickly, but she answered it nevertheless.

" Well, I do not think I am *quite* satisfied;
but I know I ought to leave the matter in the
hands of Providence."

" What is it that you do not like in your
lot as it is at present?"

"Ah, you could not comprehend it all,
Lady Halesby, if I told you," said Ellinor,
shaking her head.

" Yes, I am sure I could, and I want to
hear it."

" Well, for one thing, I do not like the idea
of having to marry for a future provision;
and you know neither Dora nor I will have
any fortunes.   I should rather be independent
of matrimony and work for myself, if there
were anything available for me to work at,"
said Ellinor, truthfully, though she had an
idea that Lady Halesby would not approve of
her independent sentiments.

Whether the latter approved or disapproved
of them, she did not say, nor did her eyes
express any feeling on the subject; but she
still held the young girl's hand in her own;
a very beautiful little hand was Ellinor's,

unadorned by a single ring; for her stock of
jewellery was extremely scanty, and rings are
not exactly a necessity in adornment.

"I told you in my note of a poor young
woman who has been ill at one of the gate-
lodges for some time," said Lady Halesby
after a pause, and lowering her voice. "She
is very reserved, but I fear sad things for her.
She is a great deal too handsome, and by no
means prepossessing. She seems a very clever
needlewoman, but I do not know what I shall
do with her when she is quite recovered. You
can walk over to the lodge to-morrow with me
and I will let you see her."

At that moment Gerard Lyon interrupted
the *tête-à-tête* by entering the room; and
Ellinor's heart beat rather quicker than before as she received his greeting. He was
very animated and in high spirits, having
just returned from a good run with the
hounds; but whether that was the sole cause
of his buoyancy is not quite certain. Lady
Halesby was very fond of her son. Providence had denied her a daughter, and all her
maternal care and love was bestowed on her
only child.

The gong for dressing soon sounded after young Lyon's arrival, and the party dispersed to their rooms to equip themselves for dinner.

CHAPTER IV.

MR. LYON WOULD LIKE TO LOOK INTO THE
FUTURE.

On a general principle, Halesby was a dull
house—in fact, an extremely dull house; and
it was rarely enlivened by company. Lord
Halesby loved agricultural pursuits, and
followed them scientifically. He made a
great many experiments in the farming line,
and sometimes succeeded, and a great deal
oftener failed, as is generally the case with
all such experiments. He spent immense
sums of money in draining certain marsh
lands, and afterwards discovered that nothing
useful or profitable would grow on them; but
he was not a penny in debt to any man or
woman. Never was there a more honourable
person, high or low, nor a better landlord.
A stout, short, pleasant-faced man he was;
proud enough at heart, perhaps, but not

D 2

ostentatious or arrogant. Going about his
park and fields in the early part of the day,
you might have mistaken him for a steward
or a head-gardener in second-best garments.
No fop was he, but he generally made himself presentadle in the evening, before dinner-
time.

His reception of Ellinor Bouverie was very
cordial—not that he cared particularly for her
above the rest of her family, as his wife did,
but because he liked the Bouveries generally,
and he was always polite to people in his own
house. It is a remarkable fact that some
people are always on better behaviour in the
houses of others than in their own; you will
find them more affable, agreeable, better
humoured, when acting as guests than as
hosts, which is contrary to the rules of hospitality, but true nevertheless. Lord Halesby
was not that sort of man. Although not, in
general, fond of visitors or company, he was
always courteous and attentive to any guests
that happened to come to the Park. He was,
on the whole, a very upright man, and a good
husband. He never interfered with his wife's
pursuits, or made objection to whatever she
chose to do. She had a private income of

her own, settled in some wonderfully strict manner on herself, so that she received it to the last penny, and spent it just as she liked. She was not a very sociable person, and she stayed a great deal in her own rooms, dining usually alone at an early hour, owing either to a real or imaginary delicacy of health, which she considered ought to prevent her keeping late hours except in the matter of breakfast, which she took very late indeed.

Upon the evening of Ellinor's arrival at Halesby, however, she appeared at the late dinner, and made a pretence of eating tiny morsels of different dishes for company's sake. There was not much conversation at table, for none of those who formed the quartette round the board happened to be very loquacious, and some way Gerard Lyon always seemed more inclined to talk to Ellinor Bouverie when other people were not listening than at other times. It so happened that they had not met since the evening of the party at Sir Ralph Barnard's, where he first was introduced to the reader, though he had dined at the general's quite lately, and there had been the Miss Skinners, and a few other ladies from the neighbourhood of Norham there, but not the Bouveries; and he had been disappointed at this, and therefore the more happy when his mother asked Ellinor down to Halesby.

"I expected to find you at Sir Ralph Barnard's, last Tuesday," he said, when dinner was over, and he joined the ladies in the drawing-room, seating himself near to Ellinor. "We had a very pleasant party there—not very many people; the Carpendales were there, and some others."

Ellinor was surprised that she and Dora had not been invited. They had not even heard before of the party; but perhaps it had been too small to ask many people to. At all events, it mattered very little now, as far as she was concerned; for the party was over, and the only person she would have cared particularly to meet at it was at the present moment talking to her. For a time she would try to cease thinking of disagreeable matters. In that large, handsome room, furnished luxuriously, with its gilt and velvet chairs, and its rare curtains, and its exquisite ornaments, and the warmth and comfort and peace reigning round her, she would endea-

vour to forget past unhappiness, if it were
possible, an give herself a little hour of
respite from care and anxiety.   Yet I am
afraid she was not altogether successful in
this effort.   Now and then a dark shadow
would cross her heart, and send a pain to her
head that made her wince and press her forehead with her hand.   A few weeks of peace
and quiet in such a house as Halesby might
certainly have the effect of calming Ellinor's
nervousness, and restoring her to a composed
frame of mind; but it was too much to expect that one day would work such an im-
provement in her mental state. A long course
of perturbation and anxiety requires much
time to cure it; and the troubles of home life
had been latterly growing far too heavy for
Miss Bouverie to bear without suffering seriously from the burthen.

"Do you remember when we used to have
such amusing games together in the shrub-
beries, and about the grounds long ago—
when Dawson and all of us were young
people?" said Gerard, after Ellinor had sat
for a long time without speaking.   "I think
we were all very happy in those days; I remember so well thinking that there never was

such a pleasant companion as your brother. I used to long so much for the time to pass quickly, when we were expecting you all down here!"

"Ah, those were happy days, indeed!" said Ellinor, as a faint flush mounted to her cheek, and she recalled the many times of old when she and Dora were staying at Halesby as children, and she had no responsibility or care weighing upon her.

"In some respects I have not altered much since that time," returned Gerard. "There are some impressions which we receive in boyhood that do not change in after years. The people whom we have valued and liked in our early years we often continue to regard with the same feelings in after life."

"Yes, very often," replied Ellinor, meeting the steady gaze of his eye, with an open, unshrinking look. "I think I still like all the people I liked, particularly in childhood."

"Do you remember the day an old fortune teller came into the grounds and prophesied very unpleasant things, because one of the gate-keepers wanted to turn her roughly away? She told me I should never have any good luck—never succeed in anything I wished particularly to succeed in—and should finally be plunged into a state of great wretchedness."

" Oh, yes," said Ellinor, laughing; " I remember it quite well."

"And you were very much distressed, and began to cry most compassionately for my future troubles."

Ellinor blushed a little, though she smiled.

" And now I am pretty old, and, as yet, none of that prophecy has been fulfilled. I have passed a very tolerable existence, and never having tried for' success in any particular undertaking, have never been disappointed."

" Ah ! but there is a long time to look forward to yet," said Ellinor, smiling and shaking her head; " you know not what the future may bring forth."

" I wish I did. In one or two respects I should like to know my future destiny—on one point especially I should be glad to read the stars correctly."

" I would not for anything hear my fortune told, even if I had perfect faith in the seership of the teller," said Ellinor, earnestly.

" Then you would not assist me in fathom-
ing the mystery of my fate ?"

" Certainly not. I always turn away from
thoughts of the future with a dread that I
cannot describe—I mean the future of this
world. The very idea of the changes that
the flight of time brings makes me shrink
back from dwelling on the years to come."

" But the changes might be very happy,"
said Gerard, looking into her clear, beautiful
eyes with a serious, contemplative expression
in his own.

" Some might, but not all; and, though I
know well that the next ten years will not
pass without bringing changes to us all, yet
as they are only vague and shadowy in our
present merciful state of ignorance of future
things, they do not occasion any defined feeling of any kind."

" You were a very clever child," said
Gerard, after he had been thinking for some
moments. " Much cleverer than Dawson or
I were. I recollect, though you were younger
than either of us, you could write much
better than we could; and when we acted
plays you understood your part always the
best. Do you recollect your having once set

up a newspaper at Halesby, and it came out
every morning to the great delight of the rest
of us? None of us knew what it contained till
its appearance in a complete form. It was about
the size of a sheet of note paper, and written
in a small hand to imitate print. I often think
now how clever it was of you at twelve years
old to act the part of editor, contributor, and
printer at the same time, and to accomplish
your daily work in about an hour each day,
shut up in the library, with the rest of
us barred out. I have one of those newspapers still, and I look upon it as a wonder
and a marvel. It contains part of a tale of
a most thrilling character, one or two reviews
of books that never existed, a murder case, a
piece of poetry, and births, deaths, and mar-
riages, besides advertisements and a very
profound leading article upon the danger to
the public of not putting a paling round a certain pond in the demesne."

"And how did you think of keeping such
a silly production?" asked Ellinor, laughing,
yet very much pleased. "I remember the
poor paper fell to the ground in less than a
week. It failed, as many of its betters have
done."

"I suppose when you went home you gave it up. I have often thought since that you must be able to write on a more enlarged scale now. You possess the same literary taste still, of course ?"

" I do not feel as energetic as I did in those days," said Ellinor, sighing in spite of herself. " The world seems very different to me now."

" And why ?"

" I had such romantic dreams at that time, such wild flights of fancy, such an ardent longing to travel to unknown regions, and roam about the world. And now, you know, those feelings have all of necessity been suppressed, and the every day affairs of life take the place of ecstatic dreamings. No one could imagine what a busy little brain I had when I was a child, sitting, perhaps, in a corner saying nothing, and taking no account of what was going on around me."

" I know that boys often have wild fancies and longings for adventure, but I did not think girls were the same," said Lyon, looking at the bright look that had come into his companion's face, with wonder and admiration.

"Oh! girls are just the same," said Ellinor, quickly. "Dora and I used both to wish ardently to travel about when we were quite little children, and see the places we read of in history, or in books of travels."

"And you never have travelled yet?"

"No; papa says he is sick of travelling and of the continent, and you know we could not well go by ourselves. Indeed, I don't know any one who would care to go abroad with us."

Ellinor was looking on the ground when she said this, half speaking to herself, so that she did not see the prolonged, peculiar look that her companion gave her as she spoke. He did not say anything for some minutes.

"I have been all over Europe," he said, at last; "yet there is much I have not seen in some of the places I have visited. I should like to go to them again, with some companion who would take an interest in the different scenes for their own sakes, and not merely for the satisfaction of saying that such and such countries had been visited."

Ellinor was still looking on the ground, thinking of her vanished childhood and its dreams that were never to be realised—of the

days gone by when she knew nothing of the
cold chains that come stealing round girls as
they gradually advance in years—till they
seem to stand manacled and fettered by some
extraordinary, incomprehensible power; and
when she raised her eyes she met such an
earnest look from Gerard's that she was surprised for a moment.   Some people fancy
they can read the meaning of all kinds of
expressions in the eye, whether of curiosity,
hatred, envy, malice, love.   Ellinor did not
pretend to any such science,   She knew that
Mr. Lyon was watching her fixedly, but with
what feeling she could not fathom.   Perhaps
he was not thinking of her at all; his thoughts
might have been far away from everything
around him.   And so, thinking this, Ellinor
met his ardent gaze with an unflinching eye,
a little sad in expression and trustful, and
very soft, but not at all embarrassed.   She
was standing near the fireplace, and he was
standing too, and the light from a branch of
candles was falling on their figures very
clearly.

Lady Halesby, watching them from a dis-
tance, where she sat in the cool air knitting at
a most elaborate piece of fancy work, thought

she had never seen her young guest look so
interesting or so graceful. Ellinor Bouverie
was remarkable for her aristocratic appearance. Very delicately formed and gentle-
looking, with an air of much quiet dignity in
the carriage of her gracefully-formed head,
you would not have seen many people like her.
Her face almost always colourless and serene,
with a look of dreamy thoughtfulness over
the clear, pale forehead, and now and then
the smile we have before mentioned lighting
it up with a pleasant burst of sunshine.
Gerard Lyon was not handsome, but he was
gentlemanly and good-looking enough. He
was frank, and of strictly honourable principles, and he had the air of self-respect which
tells of an honest heart. To some people
such a man as he was is far more attractive
than a merely handsome one. The tone of
his voice, so clear and musical—the air of
candour, and the utter absence in manner of
anything like self-sufficiency or conceit, made
him a general favourite with men as well as
women. Ellinor knew that as a boy he had
been most generous and kind-hearted, brave
and truthful—unspoiled by the indulgence of
his mother, and too goodnatured ever to

offend willingly.   If Dawson Bouverie and he
ever quarrelled in bygone days, it was always
Dawson's fault, and yet young Lyon had
always been the first to forgive and make ad-
vances towards friendship again.

As Miss Bouverie stood quietly there,
Lady Halesby got up and came towards
her.

"Ellinor," she said, "you are growing
more and more like that picture of your great
grandmother, who used to be called the
'good lady of Halesby,' whom we used to
think you like when a child.   Don't you think
so, Gerard?"

"Yes, I always thought so; but there is
nothing surprising in it.   People can be like
their grandmothers without being extraordinary," he said, laughing.

"I wish I could get a picture of you to set
beside the 'good lady,'" continued Lady
Halesby, putting her hand on Ellinor's
shoulder.   "but no painter could catch your
smile, my dear.   I daresay the 'good lady'
had your smile, too, only we cannot see it on
the canvass."

Ah! what would poor Mrs. Dart have
thought or said if she had heard that flatter-

ing speech from the usually cold, stony-eyed
Lady of Halesby ? And above all, what
would she have thought if she had heard the
few words half whispered in Ellinor's ear by
the lady's son, when his mother had moved
away again ? words that made Ellinor's face
grow first red and then paler than ever,
though there was nothing at all decided in
their significance—nothing more in them than
a very slight particle of all that was passing
in the speaker's mind. Yet Ellinor, unac-
customed though she was to construing commonplace complimentary speeches into evi-
dences of serious admiration and attachment,
could scarcely feel doubtful of their meaning,
and for a few moments she felt as if all her
presence of mind had forsaken her. She
could only collect her thoughts sufficiently to
make her endeavour to conceal her agitation
as best she might by preserving an aspect of
extreme composure and stillness. She did not
speak or look up for several minutes, and
what impression his words made Gerard could
not imagine. That they had not fallen without
observation he knew very well, by the change
in the expression of her face; but whether
she was pleased or displeased, glad or sorry,

gratified or offended, he could not clearly judge. There was a shadow on her face that scarcely spoke of pleasure; but he knew she was not indifferent, and that was a great point gained. The shadow on her face told him that; but he had no idea of the extent of the agitation Ellinor was suffering. Unstrung as her nerves had been of late by unpleasant home-scenes, perhaps any emotion might have been overpowering to her; as it was she felt quite unnerved, and she was glad when Lady Halesby, coming up again, asked her to play an air on the piano, and so gave her a reason for moving away from her former position.

Ellinor liked to play on the new grand piano at Halesby, and inspired by the tones she herself called forth, she gradually performed better and better, becoming at length lost in the charm of her own music. Extremely fond of music as he was, Gerard Lyon listened with intense pleasure to her playing, standing all the time beside her. His mother did not care particularly about general music. She loved sacred, solemn airs, and it was only lately that she presented the church at Halesby

with a magnificent organ. At her request
Elinor played some airs from Rossini's *Stabat
Mater* with such exquisite touch and expression that she entranced her listeners.   Lady
Halesby paid her many flattering compli-
ments, and Gerard praised her playing also.
Mrs. Dart would have been in agonies had
she heard the sweet words poured into Ellinor's
ears by mother and son, yet there was no fear
of her young relative becoming at all spoiled
by anything said to her.   Happy it indeed
made her to be spoken kindly to ; soothing it
was to find herself with people who said no
rude or sharp word in her presence, and who
did not mingle any bitter drop in the cup of
sweet drink presented to her ; but, though it
was pleasant to be praised and appreciated,
she was in no danger of being thrown off her
steady balance by any admiration.   For days
and weeks she had been sadly weighed down
by anxiety and care that might seem petty,
but which in reality was not so ; and now her
burthen seemed to grow less heavy, and a
faint but undefined hope of better things to
come cast a gleam of light over her mind.

It would not have been in human nature for
our young friend not to have thought in the

solitude of her room that night of the few
sentences Mr. Lyon had spoken to her, which
were certainly not without some significance.
Could it be possible that he really and seriously
cared for her? That they were very good
friends she had never doubted, and that she
had always felt for him what she considered a
most sisterly regard was certain ; but the
possibility of his thinking of her in any particularly tender light had never entered her
mind before. Gerard was not a coxcomb,
nor much given to unmeaning flirtations like
some men. He never made a practice of paying devoted attention to one girl for a time,
and then of giving her up for another, just to
gratify his own vanity. Had he been in the
habit of doing so, Ellinor would not have
taken heed of anything he said to her; but,
knowing the sort of person he was, she could
not help recalling some of his words that
night with perplexed feelings.

Was it too much for her to consider possible? Oh, could she look into the future only
this once, and read her destiny there clearly !
No, not even upon this point would she dare
to lift the veil of mystery—not dare to step
beyond the forbidden lines.

"Whatever is coming let it come," she said as she sat dreamily over the bright fire in her dressing-room, and she folded her hands resignedly together.

All her life, since very childhood, she had been accustomed to subdue all impatient feelings, all turbulent emotions, all longings for the unattainable. Few who saw her now would have believed that she had naturally been a child of strong impulses and hasty temper, early curbed by her own wisdom and by her own deep sense of what was due to others.

The next day was calm, but dull. A leaden sky hung over the outward world, but Ellinor was not in low spirits as she came down to breakfast. She tried to appear as composed as possible when she met Gerard Lyon that morning, and to look as if she had not been thinking in the least of him during the previous night. She did not mean to be a hypocrite, but women think it necessary to hide their feelings occasionally on such points as these.

This was the first time Miss Bouverie had been staying at Halesby without any other member of her family, and it was the first

time she had been asked there since Gerard
had returned from a lengthened stay abroad.
When they last met under the roof of the old
mansion he had not finished his education,
and Ellinor was scarcely grown up. Now,
then, they found a great deal to say to each
other concerning past days, which pleased
her, as she felt a shrinking from speaking of
the present—just, perhaps, because the present
was very much in her thoughts—perhaps the
present was in her companion's thoughts
also. And so they whiled away the morning,
comparing notes on books, and telling each
other how their ideas of authors and author-
ship had so much altered within the last few
years, and how their taste in literary matters
had changed too. Ellinor said that, in her
very early years, she particularly admired
descriptions of scenery and romantic incidents
in works of fiction, and that gradually her
appreciation of that sort of thing was giving
place to a more practical view of matters.
She liked descriptions of character, and
what seemed real life, now, in her reading of
fiction.

"And you were so romantic and so poetical!"
said Gerard.

"My romance is going all away," she said, smiling, but looking sad enough too. "I know a great deal more of the misery of the world now than I did then, because I go among the poor and the wretched, and I hear such tales of real, existing distress, that I do not wish to dwell on fictitious, vague melancholy. I used to imagine miseries in old times; now, I see them in reality; and— and, altogether it seems to me as if life were too sad for anyone to have need of dreamy pieces of poetry to excite melancholy feelings."

Ellinor did not say that it was scarcely necessary for her to go further than the threshold of her own home to seek for subjects likely to make her sad and thoughtful; yet something struck her companion, as she spoke, that the misery of life which she alluded to was not altogether known to her merely through the poor she visited, and a somewhat oppressive thought took hold of him, that perhaps she might have met with some disappointment in her own career Now, people generally connect only one idea with the thoughts of a disappointment in a young lady's case—that of a disappointment

in love; and as Lyon looked at her face, so
much more sad in its expression than it used
to be, a very unpleasant, painful sensation
came over him. If Ellinor had ever given
her heart away to any lover, he did not think
it likely she would take it back again as easily
as some women might. If she loved any
man once truly, she was not a person to love
another quickly, if ever again; and so, thinking this, Gerard seemed to grow dull and
posed, and Ellinor began to fear he was
getting tired of their long morning *tête-à-tête*,
which made her feel relieved when a servant
came to say Lady Halesby would be ready to
walk down to the north gate with Miss
Bouverie in about a quarter of an hour.

" Going to the gate-lodge to see her *protegée*
there, I suppose," thought Ellinor, as she went
to put on her hat, while Gerard strolled away
somewhat listlessly.

CHAPTER V.

LADY HALESBY AND HER GUEST VISIT MRS. M'STARE'S GATE LODGE.

The afternoon was grey and dull, as the morning had been. No gleam of sunshine broke over the sky, but the strong wind of the previous night had dried up the earth, and the roads were not very damp.

As Ellinor Bouverie went up to her room to get her hat, and while passing along a gallery that led to it, she observed an open letter on the ground, the handwriting of which struck her as being so like her brother's that she felt convinced she must have dropped it herself, without knowing that she had any such letter in her possession, for it was a very long time since she had heard from Dawson. Stooping to pick it up, a nearer view of the writing confirmed her in her idea of its being

her brother's, and on the side of the letter
uppermost she read these words :—

"I should be extremely obliged if you
could let me have thirty or forty pounds for a
month or so, as I expect my father to send
me some money at the end of that time, and
in the meantime I have a most confounded
and unexpected bill to pay, which—" Ellinor
thought there must be some mistake, and
stopped reading the letter which she had taken
in her hand, believing it could not be her
brother's writing, but a glance at the end
showed her Dawson's name written in full·
Like one in a trance, she read the words—
"yours very truly, my dear Lyon, Dawson
Bouverie." And then she stood for a moment or two in great wonder and perplexity,
with the blood rushing to her cheeks and
mounting up to her forehead, with a violence
that made her dizzy. She felt ashamed and
humiliated that her brother should have
asked Mr. Lyon for money. She was not
thinking of the extent of the sum, though to
her it seemed a large one, but of the bare
fact of its being borrowed from Gerard.

"Oh, he should not have done so!" she
mentally exclaimed, as, dropping the letter

where it had laid before, she hurried away, without, of course, looking at another word of it.

"Oh, if he had only borrowed it from any-one else in the whole world !" And Gerard had never mentioned this, or hinted at it to her all the previous evening or that morning. He had spoken of Dawson often with great esteem. After all, perhaps, it was not such a bad business. Young men might often borrow money from each other, and pay it again without any one wondering. Reflecting a little on the subject, Ellinor tried to grow calm and resigned—tried to banish her feeling of regret that her brother had not asked some-body else than young Lyon for money in his need. But when she got over the first sharp pangs of her misery, she began to take an-other scarcely less dark view of the case. How would her father be able to give Daw-son thirty or forty pounds to pay unexpected bills, when latterly he could not pay his own accounts, and was always hinting at a want of money ? What was to be done ?

These sort of thoughts to come haunting her even to Halesby, where she hoped to be at rest !

"Is there to be any peace for me any-

E 2

where ?" she asked herself sadly, as she put on
her hat and prepared to join Lady Halesby
for the proposed walk to the gate lodge. "Oh,
I do seem to be doomed to suffer anxiety
without end!"

"Ellinor, my, dear, you must not look so
pale," said Lady Halesby, as her guest joined
her in the drawing-room. "Really if the old
days of rouge were revived, one would
scarcely think it wrong to give you a little
colour in your cheeks."

And thus saying, she passed her hand
through Ellinor's arm, and they both left the
house.

"I do not know well what to think of the
young woman at the gate lodge," said Lady
Halesby, as they were going along. "She is
very reserved, but you can judge of her yourself."

"How is your patient to-day, Mrs.
M'Stare?" asked Lady Halesby, when they
reached the gate.

"Oh, gettin' on very well, your ladyship.
She's sittin' in the room at work," said Mrs.
M'Stare.

"I shall go in and speak to her," said
Lady Halesby.

"I think she's just well enough now to think of goin' on her way, your ladyship," observed the gatekeeper.

"We will see about that," said Lady Halesby, as she entered the lodge. Miss Bouverie followed her, and they were soon both in presence of the stranger to whom we introduced the reader some chapters ago as arriving at the quaint little residence of Mrs. M'Stare in a state of fatigue and illness, after a railway journey from Lidcombe to Halesby.

She was sitting at a little table, employed at some needlework, when the ladies entered, but she arose immediately on seeing them, and made a reverential courtesy to Lady Halesby, glancing at Miss Bouverie with eyes that did not betray much kind feeling.

"You say your name is Rebecca Hammond?" said Lady Halesby, sitting down on a small couch in the sitting-room of the lodge.

"Yes, my lady, the name I am called by," replied the young woman; and there was something in her tone that made Ellinor think it was not her real name.

"You feel, I suppose, that you would like to continue your journey to—to your friends?" said Lady Halesby, with some hesitation.

"My friends are very few," replied the girl, putting down her work, and looking with a softened expression at Lady Halesby's face. "I have no father, no mother, and no sister— scarcely a near relation in the world."

"But you seem as if you had been respectably reared," said Lady Halesby, kindly.

The young woman sighed, and went on with her work without saying anything in reply. Ellinor tried to soften her heart towards her—tried to think she was not what Lady Halesby feared she might be. She was looking at her with much pity, when the girl, raising her eyes from her work, met the earnest gaze of Miss Bouverie with a haughty glance that was not pleasant.

Ellinor would have liked to talk a little to her, but she was almost afraid to address her. Rebecca Hammond had a flashing dark eye, and a very short upper lip, prone to curl itself up, so as to look extremely short indeed; and when she chose she could look fearfully scornful. In some mysterious way Ellinor Bouverie seemed to irritate and rouse bitter feelings in her heart.

"Perhaps she thinks I do not feel kindly towards her," thought Miss Bouverie, who felt conscious of regarding the young woman with a sort of shrinking dread. " I wish I could say a few words to her alone."

Lady Halesby had a good deal to say to Rebecca, but as the latter was not disposed to be communicative she did not press her to tell anything that she seemed to wish to withhold. Mrs. M'Stare would have acted very differently in her mistress's place, and had, in fact, questioned the stranger over and over again, in a most inquisitorial manner, without gaining the slightest information as to her past life.

On rising to leave the lodge, Lady Halesby seemed puzzled as to what she should say before going away, when Rebecca, standing up, spoke herself in a tone that did not tremble in the least, though it was subdued and sad.

" You have given me shelter, Lady Halesby, for a long time, and I thank you most fervently. I am very weak still, and most wretched in every way ; but I will prepare to leave the lodge as soon as ever your ladyship thinks I should go from it. Even to-morrow I could begin my journey again."

" But do you wish to go ? Have you a friend to go to ? anybody to take care of you,

and give you protection?" asked Lady
Halesby.

"No, my lady; I fear I can reckon on no
friend half as kind, a tenth part as kind, as
yourself.   I have no purpose, no fixed plan
for the future ; but, I must go from this—I
must, indeed."

"My poor girl, you are wrong not to confide in me altogether," said Lady Halesby,
gravely ; "you may be certain that no good
can arise from your reserve; at the same time,
I am glad you do not resort to falsehood and
deception in giving a wrong account of yourself ; but you must be aware that you lay
yourself open to very serious suspicions by
refusing to speak out frankly   People are apt
to think the very worst of a young woman
who is friendless and a stranger wandering
about alone without a protector."

"What am I to understand by the 'very
worst,' Lady Halesby ?" asked the girl, as a
bright spark of excited feeling seemed to
shoot from her wild, dark eye, and a faint
colour rose to her pale face.

"The worst that can be thought of *any*
woman," replied Lady Halesby, quietly.

"Does the very worst for a woman mean

more or less than the very worst for a man,
my lady ?   Are robbery and murder among
the deepest crimes a man or woman can commit ?"

"Murder is the gravest crime of all," said
Lady Halesby, looking fixedly with her stony
eyes at her *protegée* ; "but we did not think
of imputing such to you."

"Nor robbery, my lady ?"

"No, not robbery ; nothing of that sort."

"And yet I am thought the very worst of
that could be thought of any woman, though
there have been murderers and thieves among
women ; and no one thinks me either a thief
or murderer.   What is there worse for me to
be ?"

The slight curl of the lip—the wild light
in the large eyes of the speaker—gave Ellinor
a most unpleasant feeling as she looked at
her.

Undauntedly the stranger gazed full at
Lady Halesby, with an expression that
seemed to say,

"Speak out further, if you dare !"

But Lady Halesby only looked pityingly at
her.

"I did not mean to say I thought badly of

you," she said, kindly. "I only said you
laid yourself open to very injurious suspicions
by not telling your case out frankly. Don't
you know yourself of what importance a
woman's character is to her? Surely you
have not been brought up in ignorance of
the value you ought to place on your good
name?"

" I am not ignorant of it," replied the girl,
growing calmer; "and in whatever way I
may have done wrong, I have not sunk so
low as some may dare to think. Miserable
and wretched I am, and ever must be, but
not——"

"Do not distress yourself," interrupted
Lady Halesby, who saw that the girl was
much agitated. "I am sorry I spoke as I
did ; I had no intention to offend you. For
myself I always have thought of you as well
as I could ; but I wished for some more information respecting your past life, because,
if I knew more of you, I might be able to recommend you to the notice of others."

" Thank you, my lady ; but I fear I could
not say much in my own favour, even if I
told you my whole story," said Rebecca.

Ellinor now began to regard her with feel-

ings very different from those with which she
had looked upon her at first. The shrinking
horror which she had experienced in contemplating her on her entrance to the lodge
vanished, as she felt convinced that whatever
the girl had done amiss, she had not put herself out of the pale of womanly sympathy.
She would make up her mind to seek her
confidence; she would try to win her over to
speak of her sorrows or her wrongs, and,
perhaps, she might succeed in her efforts
better than Lady Halesby had done. Ellinor
did not pause to consider that possibly Rebecca
Hammond might not be altogether truthful,
that her indignation at Lady Halesby's observations might have been feigned; yet still
she found it difficult to address her, and,
with all her good intentions, she was obliged
to accompany her hostess when she left the
lodge without saying a single kind word to
the girl.

"Well, what do you think of her?" asked
Lady Halesby, as they were out in the open
air again.

"I think she is very unhappy and very ill
still," said Ellinor.

"I am afraid she has something heavy on

her conscience," returned Lady Halesby. "Her obstinacy in maintaining such utter secrecy about her past life looks very badly."

Ellinor now found that she had forgotten her muff at the gate lodge, and as Lady Halesby sauntered slowly along she ran back for it. On entering the lodge she found Rebecca Hammond leaning her head on her hands, and giving way to a most violent outburst of grief. She did not hear the approach of the young lady, who felt for a minute or two afraid to make her presence known to her; but, summoning up courage, Ellinor at length drew near to her, and laying her hand gently on her shoulder, said—

"You must not give way to such agitation —you are not strong enough to bear it."

"Do not speak to me! do not speak to me!" exclaimed the girl, in excitement. "You cannot understand me—you can have no pity for me!"

"I have pity for you," said Ellinor, earnestly. "I wish to befriend you from my heart."

"You are happy, you are rich; you have never been poor and dependent as I have been. You can never know what it is to be friendless, and an outcast like me!"

" I know what grief and care are very well," said Ellinor, sadly ; "and I am not rich."

" Ah, yes, some little trifling grief or care you may know, but nothing of a serious kind. You have not been out upon the world since childhood, knocked about, and spurned, with never a creature to sympathise with you !"

" Confide in me," said Ellinor, impressively, as she laid her hand on the girl's shoulder. " Confide in me, and I will give you what comfort I can."

" And not despise me ?" asked Rebecca, bitterly.

" No; certainly not," replied Ellinor, who could not help feeling a return of the former shrinking horror coming over her as she said the words.

" Can I really trust you, young lady?" asked the girl.

" Yes, perfectly. I will promise even to keep your secret, so far as I can with justice to yourself and others."

" Oh! I would give the whole world to

have a true friend who would pity without
scorning me—who could make allowances for
temptation and misery, and not turn from me
in horror and disdain!"

"Make me your friend, then," said Ellinor, as she breathed a silent prayer for mercy
and forbearance in her own heart. "I promise you that you may confide most fully in
me."

"Thank you, young lady; then I will
believe and trust you, and may God bless
you."

"To-morrow, then, at about this hour, I
shall come down here," said Ellinor, hurriedly. "At present I cannot wait any
longer, but think of me till then as a true
friend."

CHAPTER VI.

NEARLY ALL ABOUT MISS BARNARD'S PRIVATE DESIGNS.

Miss Barnard was a young lady who felt perfectly satisfied with the existing customs of society. She was an only child, and she would inherit a very considerable fortune at her father's death, even if he did not choose to portion her well in his lifetime. She thought and talked by rule. She never spoke a flighty sentence, or said anything very witty or very foolish. She was one of those women who pass through life very creditably, astonishing no one by the brilliancy of her talents or the eccentricity of her behaviour. Happy would it be for many if they could follow her example and never overstep the bounds of common sense and common prejudices.

If ever she felt dubious upon any particular

point which it was the fashion to adhere strictly to, she prudently held her tongue and kept her thoughts to herself. It was wonderful how heartily she approved of everything that met the approbation of the general world. People in general said, when speaking of her, "What a nice girl Miss Barnard is," and other people answered, " Yes, *very* nice," and Miss Barnard knew they said so, and she was most polite and the most elegantly-mannered of young ladies, never seeming out of humour or without a sweet expression of countenance, except when some unimportant old lady paid her too long a visit, or some needy person came to ask assistance from the General, and upon sundry other occasions best known to the servants of her father's house. If she ever had possessed a heart she had so subdued and tutored it as to render it at the present time a very insignificant portion of her being. Every feeling was under perfect control, so that very few people, indeed, could fathom what she really thought or felt, and scarcely anyone suspected that the only fixed idea in her mind was how she could possibly best provide for her own interests and advantage. Her chief ambition at present was to secure Mr. Gerard

Lyon for her husband. Anyone else who
possessed the same advantages and equal
prospects would have answered her quite as
well. Before she ever saw him it is likely she
entertained the same designs respecting him,
and when she did see him she beheld a very
presentable, gentlemanly young man—apparently not very shrewd, or sharp, or disagree-
ably suspicious—one who might possibly fall
an easy prey to skilful managing; so he was
invited frequently to General Barnard's, and
dinner parties, with little receptions after them,
took place over and over again at Sir Ralph's
house, all for the purpose of furthering Miss
Barnard's schemes. This sounds very bad
and very worldly, does it not, reader? You
think, probably, that Miss Barnard ought to
have been quite careless as to her future
prospects—quite indifferent as to whether she
was to be plain Mrs. Somebody or a Viscountess,
or whether she remained Miss Barnard till
people said, " Really Miss Barnard is getting
quite old—quite *passée:* how odd such a nice
girl isn't married." But the young lady knew
better than that; and, therefore, to make a
long story a little shorter than it might be,
when she discovered that Mr. Gerard Lyon

would persist in hovering about Ellinor
Bouverie at the little parties at her father's
house, and *would* devote himself to her—
standing near her, even if not speaking to her,
in a manner very aggravating to Miss Barnard—that young lady determined to put
Ellinor down—and, of course, her sister down
also—and to cease inviting either of them to
the receptions of design any more.   This
determination came into her head one evening
just as she was complimenting Miss Bouverie
on her exquisite touch in the execution of a
piece on the piano, and a few minutes after
she had told Dora Bouverie that she would
give a great deal to preserve such a beautiful
delicate colour of complexion as hers was, all
through the evening in a heated room; and
the more she thought of how she would
scarcely ever again ask either of the sisters
inside her father's doors, the more sweetly and
gently she smiled upon them, and the more
composed and seraphic she looked.   Unfortunately, Gerard Lyon was not gifted with
that extraordinary insight into human character which distinguishes the favourite young
men in most novels.   He could not see through
Miss Barnard's quiet manœuvring in the least.

She was far too acute to abuse or talk slight-
ingly of any obnoxious young woman, as the
poor, clumsy Miss Skinners did. She always
admitted that pretty girls were pretty when
other people said so, and she generally added
some little flattering speech of her own to the
praises of others. She told Mr. Lyon upon
the night that she had made up her mind not
to invite the Bouveries any more that Ellinor
Bouverie was a very charming girl, and that
she liked the Bouveries greatly, and he believed her, and thought her an extremely nice
person. Miss Barnard was not at all ad-
dicted to flirting; she was far too dignified
for that, and no one ever saw her walking
out with any officers quartered at Norham,
even when accompanied by her father. Altogether she was a most properly-behaved young
lady, whom many a man considered would
make the best of wives; but she was as cold
as an icicle to every admirer—cold and suave,
and polite and self-possessed, till half a dozen
of them were nearly at their wits' end with
distraction. She felt no emotion of pleasure
at their homage, for she was not a coquette;
she had no pity or sympathy for them; and
a few whose proposals she was obliged to re-

fuse received answers spoken in the best-
chosen language, without a word out of place,
or a tone not properly modulated. She had
the sweetest of voices, always under perfect
control ; never faltering, or becoming unclear
from emotion; and with this low, soft voice
she dismissed her lovers in elegant, and often
in complimentary phrases, declaring she would
esteem them (the poorer they were the more
emphatically she would esteem them), and expressing a fervent hope that they would soon
forget her, caring very little at the same time
whether they did or not, and thus getting rid
of the deluded creatures without suffering the
slightest pain herself.

Sir Ralph Barnard was by no means sorry
that his daughter chose to exclude the young
ladies at Evergreen from the ensuing parties
at his house. He was beginning to have
fears about his aide-de-camp, Mr. St. George,
falling in love with Dora Bouverie, and he
liked the young man well enough to wish to
preserve him from any possible chance of
making a bad matrimonial speculation. The
penniless Dora Bouverie, with her beauty and
her propensity to captivate nearly every
second man of her acquaintance, who was not

previously provided with the safeguard of a
wife, or a prior attachment, was a dangerous
creature, and it would be well to keep her
out of the way of a young man whose
bounden duty it was to look out for a wife
with money.

Thus it was satisfactorily arranged that
the Bouveries were not to be admitted in
future to the parties at Sir Ralph Barnard's.

The next people who determined to put the
Miss Bouveries down were the Skinners, mother
and daughters, who had been struggling to
keep their necks above the obscurity of
acknowledged poverty for the last ten years
—ever since the head of the family, John
Skinner, died, leaving three women who had
full possession of their mental faculties and
uncommonly good appetites, reduced to a state
of great privation. John Skinner had enjoyed
a government pension upon retiring from a
lucrative appointment which he had held for
several years, and which gave him hardly
anything to do; and, of course, when he
dropped into the grave the pension dropped
too, and poor Mrs. Skinner, who used to get
good things to eat and good clothes to wear as

long as her husband lived, found herself
obliged to put up with very scanty, coarse
fare, and very shabby garments, as soon as
he was taken from her. She was not burnt
like a Hindoo widow, to enable her to enjoy
speedy happiness in the next world. She was
only half-starved and pinched in circumstances for the remainder of her life in this
world, and she would have been a most
afflicted, inconsolable widow, shutting herself up in retirement (for being past sixty she
did not think it likely she could get another
husband) had it not been for her daughters,
for whom she entertained hopes of advancement in life, and for whose sake it
was necessary not to be afflicted,
and not to waste time in a long retirement. She had also a son, regarding whom
she entertained that superstition so popular
among men and women, that he would be of
great advantage to her and his sisters at some
future period of his existence, and mother
and sisters looked upon him as a wonder
among human beings. A sharp, selfish rude
youth he was, spoiled and pampered, taking
his mother's and sisters' homage and atten-

tion as things of course, and therefore not to
be regarded with gratitude or thankfulness.
The three women pinched and starved themselves to get Jack Skinner on in the world,
and to enable him to complete his education
—not altogether for his own sake, perhaps,
but most probably also with an eye to some
advantage for themselves. Jack got the best
food and the best clothes that could be procured by the united efforts of the mother and
sisters, and consequently he despised his
female relatives, and was very discontented
that he had not more money, and was obliged
to work for a livelihood. Now, like his elder
sister, Jack had great acuteness and a great
deal of cunning, which he could fortunately
turn to better account than she could, for I
do not suppose that she ever gained more
than a few pence after a whole day's wrangling and bargaining with a shopkeeper;
whereas her brother's sharpness was of tremendous advantage to him in the line of life
he adopted. He became a barrister, after a
great deal of study and perseverance on his
own part, and much expense to his mother;
and was now settled in London, doing a great

deal of business, and supposed to be on the
way to much wealth and fame. Mrs. Skinner still preserved her superstition that he
was of advantage to her, though she only
saw him about once in two years, when he
would run down from town for a day or two,
taking a return ticket for the railway fare ;
for he was very prudent and economical, and
so busy he could scarcely spare a moment
for leisure. Now, when a man of business,
and especially a man of the law, is overwhelmed with work, people generally suppose him to be very rich ; for, on a general
principle, men do not work for nothing, and
therefore Mrs. Skinner delighted to tell people
how very busy John was, and how much respected he was, and what a successful barrister he was—"gaining nearly every cause he
took in hand, and sought after by everyone."
She exaggerated a good deal, poor soul; but
all her pride was centred in this son, who
never gave her any assistance out of his
abundance, except perhaps a present of a new
gown, worth about three guineas, or a shawl
of even less value, at times few and far between. I think, however, that the sisters of

this thriving barrister had begun to give up
their superstition respecting his superhuman
qualities.

Time was bringing an increase of money,
and consequently an increase of worldly respect to Jack Skinner, and it was bringing
an increase of years, and consequently an increase of worldly contempt to his sisters.
What wonder, then, if the latter were soured
and ill-tempered? What wonder that Miss
Skinner, in an hour of desperation, as she
contemplated the wretchedness of limited
means, determined that she would settle in
life at last, and begin to look favourably on
a certain Mr. Dozyhead, a gentleman of good
income, who had for a great many years admired her without meeting with much en-
couragement from the lady. His income
was considerable, but his intellect and morals
were very low indeed. He was scarcely ever
sober, and he had the reputation of being
half silly. At the same time he was invited
to all the festive gatherings round Norham,
and looked upon as a very desirable *parti* by
such people as had no serious objection to
dissipated habits and a want of wisdom in

men. Miss Skinner strongly disapproved of the new idea that women should have professions, and fully believed that it would destroy their refinement and delicacy if permitted to work like men for their own independence and advancement in life; but she did not think there was anything particularly unrefined in the idea of marrying a man whom she despised, and probably disliked, merely because his money would enable her to maintain a good position in society.

CHAPTER VII.

CAPTAIN BOUVERIE HAS A PARTICULAR POINT
TO GAIN.

ONE day Mr. Clarke called at Evergreen, and
knowing, as she did, by the peculiarly loud,
sudden ring of the door bell, who the visitor
was, Dora immediately left the drawing-room
and took refuge in her own room, intending
not to leave it till the barrack-master was
gone; but to her surprise her father came upstairs and requested her to make her appearance in the drawing-room.

" But, papa, I have no wish to see Mr.
Clarke," said Dora, trying to speak carelessly,
and pretending to be absorbed in reading a
book she had just snatched up from the
table.

" But I wish you to see him," returned her
father, rather emphatically.

" Then I am not dressed, and I have so

F 5

much to do downstairs," said Dora, rather
more softly than she would have spoken had
she not observed how anxious, and even distressed, her father looked. " I really must
be excused, papa, for not appearing to visitors
to-day—at this hour, at least."

" Never mind your dress; you are very
neat, and you always look pretty; come down,
my dear, when I ask you," said Captain
Bouverie, putting his arm round his daughter
very affectionately.

" I should much rather not go down, papa;
indeed I should. Mr. Clarke cannot wish to
see me; it is quite impossible he can have
anything particular to say to me."

" But it seems rude, my dear, for the ladies
of the family to make a point of not appearing to the gentlemen who call at the house."

" Really, papa, I do not think so ; I know
several houses where Ellinor and I visit, and
the gentlemen of the families never think of
coming in to see us."

" Ah! that is a different affair; men are
always busy, and perhaps generally out of
doors, but ladies are supposed to be at home,
and to have nothing particular to occupy
them."

"I wish I had told Patty to say I was out," said Dora, who was growing impatient and nervous. "Do go downstairs, papa, or that horrible man will wonder where you are."

"He knew I came up here for you, Dora," said Captain Bouverie, frowning slightly; "and I do not intend to go down again without you."

"Well, then, I must really say you have very little regard for my wishes, papa," said Dora, flushing. "I particularly dislike Mr. Clarke, and I am afraid if I meet him I shall let him see it."

"My dear girl, you do not know what you are saying," said Captain Bouverie, bitterly, and a little sadly, too. "Clarke has been a good friend to me, and I am sure you would not like to make him an enemy."

"Tell me what he has done for you, papa, and then I will judge if he really is a friend."

"Take my word for it that he is a friend, and that he has a great deal in his power, Dora. There, now, I know you are a good girl; you will come down and gratify me will you not?"

Captain Bouverie stooped down and kissed his daughter's cheek very paternally, and she

felt mollified, yet still so wretched that tears
came into her eyes. With some of her old
feelings of coquetry, she was about to
give her hair a few improving brushes, when,
turning suddenly from the toilet glass, she
forbore to add to her attractions in the least.

"There now, papa; I am ready to go
down," she said, in desperation. "But remember I only go because you ask me.
Nothing will ever make me think well of Mr.
Clarke himself."

The father felt bitterly, and sighed; but he
had gained his point so far, and perhaps he
would yet gain it further.   Dora was not
obstinate, and she would yield to kindness
and affectionate persuasion when she would
resist tyrannical oppression.   It is generally easy to persuade or oblige women to
comply with the wishes of those who hold
power over them; so thought Captain
Bouverie. They are too dependent to strive
long against any mandate, however disagreeable, if it be persisted in and enforced without flinching. They have nowhere to fly to
from domestic tyranny, and the world looks
coldly and doubtfully on any of them who
try to break their chains. Perhaps the

captain felt glad his daughters were dependent upon him. It is a consolation often to a tyrannical person to know that even an insignificant creature is in his power, ready to be crushed if he will.

Very insignificant, indeed, had this father considered his daughters till a few weeks ago, when he first began to think one or other of them might be made useful to him. There are good fathers in the world, who will scarcely understand the sort of man Captain Bouverie was; and there are bad fathers—worse even than he was—brawling and dishonourable and brutal. Captain Bouverie rarely said or did anything ungentlemanly. In his most enraged moments he scarcely ever made use of an oath or a profane expression of any kind; and as to lifting his hand to strike anyone—such an idea never entered his head: yet still he was an unmitigated domestic tyrant—offensive to the last degree. At the same time he held liberal political views, and was, in profession, almost a thorough Radical. Being a younger son of limited income, he considered that the aristocracy should be put down, and even that a republic would be more advantageous to England than a monarchy. Nothing would

have reconciled him to royalty and the aristocracy but to make him the King himself, or,
at least, a peer of the realm. Hating rule and
authority over himself, he carried out whatever of authority the law permitted him to
hold in his own hands with an astonishing
degree of rigour, as his wife and daughters
knew but too well. In this respect he re-
sembled that poetical tyrant, Milton, whose
name and character every woman should abhor.

Coming into the drawing-room, with a
feverish spot glowing on her cheek, and a
bright light burning in her eye, Dora advanced to greet Mr. Clarke with a coolness of
manner that did not quite coincide with her
flushed appearance. The hand that she gave
him was burning and trembling, and yet her
voice was steady, though not very audible.
Within the last few days her nerves had been
more tried than they had ever been in her life
before. Naturally she had not weak nerves
—but continual torment will gradually shake
the strongest ; and she was, at last, beginning
to understand that miserable feeling of nervousness which so many women are plunged
into by the uncertainty and discomfort of their
social position.

Mr. Clarke was a man whose nerves were very strong indeed, and whose penetration enabled him to see through Dora's forced calmness, though it did not enable him to comprehend the full extent of her feelings towards himself.   His large, muscular hand seemed to swallow up the young girl's in a grasp strong and firm, and he looked into her eyes, which had of late lost their expression of careless happiness, with an unshrinking gaze, perhaps a little triumphantly too.

" You must feel lonely, now, without your sister," he said, when the first salutation was over.

" Yes, very lonely.   It is almost the first time we were separated," replied Dora, trying for her father's sake to speak civilly, for she saw that he was watching her with anxiety.

" She is enjoying her visit to Halesby, I hope ?"

" I really do not know.   It was one of our agreements that neither of us was to write to the other all the time she was away, unless something extremely important were to happen at home or at Halesby."

" That must have been quite a sacrificial ar-

rangement, considering the love of letter-
writing most young ladies possess."

" Oh, I have no love of the kind," said
Dora; " I never write to any one, and I never
get letters."

" *Le bon temps viendra*," returned the barrack-master, looking admiringly at Dora's
beautiful golden hair, which the winter sun
was lighting up brightly, though it was not
quite smooth.

" I hope not, if you mean that the good
time is to be when I am under the necessity
of writing and receiving letters. I should
prefer having any friends I particularly care
for always near enough to prevent the necessity of an exchange of letters."

" But that would be impossible, I fear.
Even husbands and wives are often separated,
and obliged to speak to each other by pen and
ink."

" And I dare say they do not quarrel as
frequently then as when speaking by word of
mouth."

" That may be, certainly. But I hope you
do not consider quarrelling the inevitable result of matrimony ?"

"I am afraid it is a very common one," said Dora, shaking her head.

"My dear Dora, you surely do not mean what you say?" observed Captain Bouverie.

"Indeed I do, papa," replied our heroine, frankly. "I am sure I should quarrel dreadfully, and make the very worst wife anybody ever had."

The father pretended to laugh good humouredly, as he patted his daughter's cheek, but he did not feel really at ease.

"You exaggerate your faults, my dear," he said, pleasantly, "and I must in justice say you have proved yourself far superior to even what I had expected of you since Ellinor's departure. No one could better perform the part of housekeeper which has now devolved upon you than you have done, and that is an essentially feminine accomplishment."

Dora felt surprised, and looked wonderingly at her father.

"It is a part I thoroughly detest!" she said emphatically. "So I am afraid I cannot put in my claim to being truly feminine. I hope I may never be obliged to be my own housekeeper ; that is all. I should infinitely prefer living like an anchorite on nuts, and fruits, and frugal fare, to taking any trouble about more elaborate provision."

Mr. Clarke smiled. He cared very little whether the young lady liked or disliked managing a household. It is only men who go soberly and practically about looking for wives that pause to weigh very carefully the merits of the ladies they intend to honour with their choice. Dora Bouverie might curl her lip in contempt, or smile most sweetly— it was pretty much the same to her admirer. In his eyes she was beautiful, whether angry or pleased; and as to her temper or mental qualities, they were of very minor importance at present. Perhaps he considered that it would be in his power to break the spirit of anyone—man or woman—who was thoroughly dependant upon him, in a very short time. A woman especially can be easily subdued and broken in, with the law and the world against her, and nowhere for her to turn to for refuge when once she is fairly entrapped and enslaved. If home and husband are disagreeable, she cannot go off to a club and stay there, or roam about gossiping through town, and so escape all day from torment and tyranny. The wiser she is the more she will feel the prudence of bearing her chains with a good grace, when once she has agreed to wear them. But let her reflect a good deal, if she can afford to do so, before slipping on the bonds that are so hard to slip off again—in fact, so impossible to escape from, except by death, or a sad shipwreck of peace and credit and honour, more fearful than death.

" My little Dora is not quite so bad as she represents herself," said Captain Bouverie, who found it difficult to repress the dark frown that was struggling to reach his forehead. "She would be the best girl in the world if she would only learn how to speak a little less at random."

Could it be possible that her father was turning so mean as to cringe to that terrible man, Mr. Clarke ? Could it be possible he was contemplating some frightful sacrifice for the propitiation of this barrack-master whom Dora so thoroughly detested? The thought came into her head, and she turned an unconsciously reproachful look at her father's face—a look so sad and bitter, and almost contemptuous, that Mr. Clarke remarked it, and almost understood it in its true light. The world of Nor-

ham knew pretty well that Captain Bouverie
was not a particularly tender father, as far as
regarded his daughters; and, perhaps, Mr.
Clarke knew it better than most people, and,
perhaps, he speculated somewhat upon that
very knowledge.

"I wish you would go out, Dora, and buy
something I want," said Captain Bouverie,
when Mr. Clarke was about to take his departure. "A walk will be of use to you, and as
I have not time to go out, my friend here will
escort you to the town."

"Oh, thanks, papa, I can go alone without
troubling Mr. Clarke," was the incorrigible
Dora's reply. "I am not ready to go out at
present, and I should not like to keep Mr.
Clarke waiting."

"Nothing would please me better than to
wait upon you, I assure you," said the barrack-master, with earnestness.

"Go and get your bonnet, Dora," said
Captain Bouverie, in a tone of firmness and
command which his daughter understood perfectly, though an indifferent hearer might not
have remarked it particularly.

"I should much prefer going out later in
the day," remonstrated Dora.

"But you see I want paper and pens, and
—and some other things *immediately*," said
the father, rather at a loss to know what he
had best want particularly, as he turned a
somewhat threatening eye on his daughter's
face.   She returned his look with a very reproachful one, but felt obliged to obey him,
not that she was afraid of him, but she pitied
him, while she wondered at him.

When she left the room to get her bonnet
he followed her, and, taking her by the arm
in a nervous, hurried way, impressed upon
her the necessity of being polite to Mr. Clarke.

"I observe a great tendency to treat him
with flippancy," he said, seriously, "and I
cannot permit it.   I suppose, Dora, you have
some regard for your father and for your
brother?"

"Yes, of course, papa; but what has Dawson to do with the matter between you and
Mr Clarke?   I have certainly a great regard
for you, but I am afraid my brother has not
earned much from me.   He never did anything but tease me that I can remember."

"Come, come, no trifling, please.   Brothers
have all a right to consideration and respect
from their sisters."

"Not unless they deserve it, papa. I am
not going to believe that I owe any sacrifice
whatever to Dawson, I assure you," said
Dora, who entertained a very clear recollec-
tion of her brother's rude speeches and
disobliging manners during the past years of
his life.

"You have been brought up very badly,
Dora," declared her father, frowning now to
his heart's content, when no stranger was
present.

"An eye for an eye, and a tooth for a
tooth," said Dora, turning her provoking blue
eyes on her father's dark and troubled visage,
as she fled upstairs lightly of foot, but very
heavy at heart, and perplexed and afraid to
dwell very much upon what her father
really wished to be the end of this civility to
Mr. Clarke.

"I would wear the very ugliest bonnet I
have," she said, as she prepared to put on the
most becoming little hat that ever was seen,
"only that I might meet some one whose
opinion might be of consequence to me," and,
therefore, she adjusted the said hat in an
extremely coquettish manner, and put on her
best velvet cloak, and her smallest boots, and

an exquisite little pair of gloves, so that her
father was quite pleased at her appearance
when she came downstairs, not knowing
that she had dressed herself thus becomingly
for other eyes than those of the barrack-
master.

" Now you are quite blooming," said Captain
Bouverie, smiling fondly.

" Most charming !" said Mr. Clarke.

" I wish I was hideous !" exclaimed Dora,
impatiently, at which strange speech both
her papa and her admirer laughed pleasantly.
Everything she said seemed so very amusing
to them at present; and I believe if she had
got the wish so expressed, she might have
been a far happier young woman than she
was, or ever had been.

" People will think we are going to be
married now," said Mr. Clarke, as he and
Dora were walking together towards the
town.

" Oh ! no ; they would not imagine anything so absurd," was the young lady's
doubtful rejoinder. Some weeks ago such an
answer as that would have cast him down
considerably; but he did not feel so sensitive
and humble now. He had an ally at present

more powerful far than the girl herself, and he
felt aided and abetted to the utmost.

" Gossips do not weigh the absurdity of the
reports they spread," he said.

" But they would scarcely spread a report
which could not have the slightest foundation," observed Dora, speaking with apparent
carelessness.

" And why should it not have a foundation?" asked the barrack-master softly.

" Simply because it has not," replied Dora,
trying to speak with unconcern, though her
heart began to sink very unpleasantly.

A pause of some minutes now took place
in the conversation, but, instead of giving our
heroine any composure of mind, it only in-
creased her perplexity.

" You must know, Miss Bouverie, how
much I admire you," said her companion,
breaking the dreadful silence, with words
very like what she dreaded to hear. " I more
than admire you, for a feeling towards you
far deeper than admiration has of late occupied my whole heart, and I have reason to
believe that your father looks favourably on
my attachment."

" And you mentioned it to him first ?" said

Dora, roused suddenly out of her nervous
embarrassment, as she cast a reproachful look
at her companion.

"Pardon me if I have offended, but I
thought it the best way to consult with
Captain Bouverie before presuming to address
yourself."

"I am sorry you did so," she said,
"especially as he approves of what you
said to him, for I fear he may be disappointed."

"Miss Bouverie, are you really so bereft of
feeling as to speak so? If anyone is to suffer
disappointment of a most bitter kind, it must
be myself, should you not accept the proposal
which I would make with the most ardent
feelings of devotion. Your father's sentiments
on the subject will be very faint, indeed, com-
pared to mine."

"I wish you had never thought of me in
such a light," said Dora, almost humbly, as
she remembered with penitent feelings much
unmeaning coquetry on her own part towards
the man who was now making her miserable
by his declaration of love. "I could not
make you happy—indeed I don't think I
could make any one happy. I am selfish and

ill-tempered and full of faults, and I never
could return the sentiments you express for
me, in the slightest degree. Indeed I think I
have no heart. You have no idea of what a
useless, unamiable creature I am."

" You undervalue yourself altogether. At
all events, I should be quite willing to persist in what I have said, if you were a hundred
times more unamiable than you represent
yourself. Nothing can change my sentiments
towards you now."

" So much the worse," said Dora, who was
in too great fear as to what her father might
say to her, to experience any of the usual
embarrassment attending such a position as
her present one was. Terror of her father
overcame all other feelings.

" You will think over this," said Mr.
Clarke, who was able to speak pretty coolly;
"you cannot mean to cast me into utter
misery without a moment's reflection."

" I will promise to think over it," replied
Dora, catching at a straw of hope on the wild
sea she seemed cast into, " if you also make
me a promise ;" and she looked into his face
with sad, beseeching eyes, unaware herself of
how anxious and pale she looked.

"I will promise anything you ask."

"Then you must promise not to say any-thing to papa of what you have mentioned to me since we came out, till I can give you my-self a definite answer," she said.

"But how long am I to wait for the defi-nite answer?" asked the barrack-master, with his usual regard to calculation.

"I cannot tell you that; it must depend on circumstances ; but I do not like to make papa anxious on the subject. You will pro-mise me, will you not ?"

And so it had come to this. Dora was obliged to ask a favour very humbly of the person whom she used to despise and dislike. Was it a punishment for her sins of heartless-ness and cruel coquetry practised on so many unhappy beings during the last two years? Perhaps it was. Had she ever felt so wretched in her whole life, as she did at that moment? She thought she had not.

"I wish I did not care so much as I do for papa," she thought ; "for if I did not, how easily I could give my answer to Mr. Clarke; yet still my answer must be the same, first or last. No reflection can possibly alter my de-termination as it stands at present."

Dora Bouverie was no longer the merry, thoughtless girl of two months ago ; but, unlike her sister, her newly-acquired thoughtfulness was not so much for others as for herself. Unfortunately it appeared to her just now, as if she herself, of all the people ever she knew, stood the most in need of her utmost care and anxiety ; and perhaps she was right, for truly she stood on the edge of a dark precipice, over hanging very dark depths below.

" You will promise, will you not ?" she said, in a low, subdued voice.

" For how long am I to be thus bound ?" asked her companion.

" Till I have quite made up my mind."

He looked at her rather distrustfully. Her manner, so different from what it used to be, puzzled him ; but it might be better to grant her the promise she asked. Would he not have given something of far greater value to secure one kind thought from her ? But this promise was not an easy one to make.

Captain Bouverie's influence in his family must be powerful ; he was a man of strong self-will ; he was the head of his household— the ruler of his home ; wife and daughters must be dependent on him, and being de-

pendent, they must submit to his decrees. To
lose his help and alliance might be very
prejudicial to the cause the barrack-master
had so much at heart ; and probably Dora
knew this, and had hopes of escaping her
father's persuasions and commands ; yet still
he must try and please her by granting her
request, and so with a good grace he did so,
and she was satisfied.

Passing on to the town, Dora tried several
times unsuccessfully to shake off her companion, but having got her father's permission
to walk with her, he was not going to relinquish the privilege quite so soon as she
wished ; and she was obliged at length to
pretend she wanted particularly to call on the
Skinners as an excuse for getting rid of him ;
so, of course, he had to leave her at the door
of Mrs. Skinner's shabby house ; and she was
glad to spend twenty minutes listening to the
poor old lady's rambling conversation, because her visit afforded her respite from Mr.
Clarke's attentions. Mrs. Skinner was suffering from a severe attack of rheumatism, in
consequence of having been obliged to *chaperon* her daughters to a ball thirteen miles

from Norham a few nights before, when the
snow lay several inches thick on the ground ;
and to-day the daughters were out on an
expedition of search for somebody to *chaperon*
them to another party, since their mother was
put *hors de combat.*

"I hope they will get Mrs. Sillybrains to
take my place," said Mrs. Skinner, unable to
suppress a sudden exclamation of pain, as
she moved her neck and head in addressing
Dora, who thought Mrs. Sillybrains, who was
just eighteen, and had been married six
months ago, rather a funny substitute for
Mrs. Skinner as matron to her daughters,
whose years very nearly numbered twice the
amount of their proposed *chaperon.*

"I wish Charlotte was married, if it was
only to go about to parties with Minnie,"
continued the poor suffering mother. "It is
so unpleasant, you know, having to ask
strangers to matronise you. The two girls
are hunting about all day for some one to
take them to the ball to-night, and really if
they can get nobody else, I must make an
effort and go with them myself. Dear, dear!
how dreadful this rheumatism is!"

"What a pity it is they cannot go by themselves," said Dora.

"By themselves!" repeated Mrs. Skinner, bridling, and looking very doubtfully at her young visitor.

"Yes; I should much prefer going to a party alone, to letting mamma get her death of cold coming with me," said the young lady frankly.

"Oh! I am glad to say my young people don't entertain *those* kind of independent ideas," observed Mrs. Skinner, with dignity. "Oh-h-h, what a twinge!"

"You are really very ill," said Dora compassionately; and, having a great dislike to seeing anyone suffering, she took the earliest opportunity of escaping from her old friend in order to spare herself any further pain. And now she was alone and free as far as the present was concerned. Getting out of Mrs Skinner's narrow hall and narrow hall-door, she walked up the narrow but highly-respectable street where the house was situated; for Norham had its particular *quartiers* of old traditional respectability and extreme dinginess, in contradistinction to

more snobbish *locales* where the houses were
large, and airy, and newly built, and very
handsome, but where nobody who had the
slightest claim to fashion or good birth would
live upon any consideration.   Dora Bouverie
was going along, thinking how the future
might turn out for her, when just at the top
of the street she met Mr. St. George, dressed
in his military uniform.

CHAPTER VIII.

MR. ST. GEORGE SPEAKS OUT RATHER PLAINLY.

DORA greeted the apparition of Mr. St. George with the brightest smile her face had worn for many days—a beaming smile of surprise and pleasure—because the meeting was too sudden and unexpected to cause her any embarrassment. Besides, she felt in a great measure carried far beyond minor feelings at present by the tremendous nature of her late interview with Mr. Clarke, which had borne her away from all trifling considerations.

" It is a long time since I saw you," he said, as she stopped and shook hands with him.

" Yes; I have not been out for many days, and my sister has been away."

" And do you never go out without your sister?" he asked, wondering if Ellinor Bouverie's absence from home had anything to do

with Dora's non-appearance of late at the
parties at General Barnard's.

" Oh, yes! sometimes ; but her being away
makes a great difference to me."

And now, of course, Mr. St. George considered it his bounden duty to turn and escort
his fair friend for at least some part of the way
she was pursuing; and though he observed
that she was a little subdued, and not disposed to talk in as lively a manner as of old,
he did not regard her as at all less interesting in
her new character. Indeed, perhaps, he regarded her as more so. But this was not
wonderful, for when a man once admires a
woman very much he generally considers
every new phase of manner charming ;
whether she is merry or grave, joyous or sad,
it is all pretty much the same. He rarely
thinks her gaiety folly, or her silence stupidity,
whatever opinion other mortals may be disposed to entertain on the subject. Not having seen Dora Bouverie for several days—and
her absence at the evening parties of Sir
Ralph Barnard's—caused Mr. St. George to
regard this meeting as a particularly fortunate
one. He had been on duty in the morning,
and was returning to his quarters to divest

himself of his military garments, when he met the young lady.

"I was beginning to think Norham extremely stupid for the last three or four days," he said, as they walked together.

"Why, I heard you had some delightful parties last week and this week at Sir Ralph's," observed Dora.

"To me they were stupidity itself," he said. "Other people may have found them pleasant enough, perhaps ; but you ought to know, Miss Bouverie, that there could have been no attraction there for me."

"How could I know? I have not even heard whom the parties consisted of."

"But you know some who were *not* there?"

"Oh, yes, certainly. For instance, I know I was not there myself."

And Dora laughed a little innocent laugh, apparently most guileless and careless.

"You speak so indifferently!" said St. George, looking at her reproachfully.

"But how can I speak otherwise? You do not trust me ; you do not say why you found Sir Ralph's last parties so dull."

" And you cannot possibly know the reason yourself ?"

" Really you seem to imagine that I am gifted with a spirit of divination."

" No; but I can scarcely believe that you are so unobserving as not to understand by this time why I should consider any place dull where *you* were not present."

This was pretty plain speaking ; but our heroine was still too much carried away from common feelings by her recent meeting with Mr. Clarke to feel as she would have done had her companion spoken to her in this way a week ago, or even the day before. So much emotion of an unpleasant kind had been experienced by her during the interview she had just passed through, that she found it almost impossible to be moved deeply now. Perhaps she had some passing idea that what her present companion was saying to her, or would ever say to her, could be of no consequence to her any more in this life. And yet she spoke and laughed so lightly, that no one could have suspected what a chill, dark feeling had settled over her heart for the last hour or two.

" Did you really regret my being absent from any party lately ?" she asked, turning her eyes on his face with an earnest, serious expression.

" Yes, I really did; in fact, I was perfectly wretched."

" But this is only a fleeting fancy on your part. It will pass away, and it will be better for you that it should," said Dora, who was not speaking carelessly now. Usually, when any admirer was approaching a declaration of attachment to her she pretended not to understand what he was trying to aim at, and so spared herself the disagreeable necessity of informing him she could not return his love, &c. She was a great coquette and a heartless one, on a general principle, but she did not wish to cause Mr. St. George any unnecessary pain.

Now, Mr. St. George felt that he had already said a good deal of a pretty decisive character, and, though he knew he might be placing himself in a difficult position, he believed that for his own happiness he might as well speak out further, and tell his companion the full extent of his feelings towards her.

It seemed a singular coincidence that on the same day Dora Bouverie was destined to listen to two declarations of love from different people, one of whom she regarded with greater dislike than almost any one she ever knew, the other of whom she felt very differently towards, indeed.

"You do not know, perhaps," she said, speaking so calmly that her companion might have augured badly from it for any success he hoped for, "that I can have no fortune, that my father's income is not large, and that I am afraid (but this is confidential) that he has become involved in some pecuniary difficulties of late."

Mr. St. George said that no worldly considerations could alter his feelings towards her now ; his own income was not large, nor was there much likelihood that it ever would be, although, of course, promotion in his profession might be looked forward to if he continued in the army. He said nothing of any prospect that existed of his ever inheriting his uncle's titles or estates. The dream of ever being Viscountess Killevan in the peerage of Ireland would possibly never be realised for Dora; yet, still there was a feeling in her heart deeper than any connected with that disappointment. She was sorry Mr. St. George was not a wealthy person, because there might then be an end to her own and her father's perplexities, and she might feel that she was shielded from the dark misery that she seemed journeying towards so rapidly now.

"I am very much flattered and gratified that you like me," she said, a little sadly; "and yet I am sorry, too, for I am afraid it would be imprudent for you to think of me in any other light than that of a friend."

"You are afraid to venture to try for happiness on a small income?"

"Not for myself; but I do not like to be the means of dragging you down in the world; you deserve a better fate; you are worthy of a wife who would be a help rather than an embarrassment to you. You do not know what a worthless creature I am. I hardly know what I am myself; for it is only within a very short time that I have troubled my brain with any reflections at all. I have not been very happy since I was a child, and I have always, since I grew up, tried to banish thought as much as possible, because there was nothing pleasant for me to think about. I have been vain and silly, because I had no other amusement than what the gratification of vanity gave me. You do not know what monotonous lives the generality of women lead; and if you take away the pleasure they have in frivolity, and gaiety, and vanity, there would be nothing at all left but what was dull and sad. Just fancy living from year's end to year's end in a place like Norham, and having no occupation of an interesting kind, and feeling that, as time passes, you will be even more dull and more monotonous, with no amusement at all."

"But it is very unlikely you will live at Norham much longer. Even if you reject me, you will surely marry some one else who may take you from this neighbourhood."

They were now in the middle of the chief street of Norham, and Sir Ralph Barnard, riding on horseback, met them in full face, having seen them long before they saw him, for the General had very quick sight, and was very sharp in a great many ways. No manœuvring, match-making mamma was ever more acute in the matter of detecting a court-

ship or a flirtation than this excellent veteran.
He had already, however, prevented more
matches than he had forwarded, his opinion
being that men were happier in a single state
than married, and that the longer they put
off the terrible ordeal of matrimony the better it would be for them.

He returned Dora's salutation with courtesy,
but gave a look at her companion that plainly
said, "1 see the case is nearly hopeless;
something must be done to save you."

Mr. St. George saluted him gravely, but
the colour rose very perceptibly to his face,
while Dora betrayed no emotion at all. She
did not blush in the least; she was not thinking of what Sir Ralph's sentiments were, nor
indeed of what any gossip at Norham might
be surmising. She felt very strangely; not
as she used to do. It seemed to herself as if
she had grown quite old and changed within
the last few days.

The General stopped his horse, and spoke
to his aide-de-camp. He said he would be
particularly obliged if he would execute some
commission for him, which he invented on
the spot, and of course the young man had to

say he would be happy to do it. It was
something that had to be done immediately,
and there was only time to say good-bye to
Dora, and to hurry away.

During her solitary walk home the young
girl felt very thoughtful—nearly bewildered.
That winter day had been very eventful to
her—almost terrible as regarded Mr. Clarke's
proposal; for she knew that her father sanc-
tioned and approved of him, and she also
knew that he would not look favourably on
his rival.

" What a dreadful thing it is to be poor,"
she thought; " and what a sad world it is
where we cannot do without money. I myself have always been so mercenary and discontented with our limited income; and yet,
perhaps, the want of money has not been the
sole cause of our unhappiness at home.
People might be happy enough on small
means if there were nothing else to make them
wretched."

After all, it was not so much the want of
money as the mismanagement of what there
was that caused embarrassment at Evergreen.
There was great extravagance on Captain

Bouverie's part in some ways, and of course much saving and pinching to make up for unnecessary expenses.

Dora began to think that if her father and mother had truly loved each other, and sympathised fully with each other, there might have been more domestic peace and cheerfulness in the family. Poverty need not make people's tempers irritable or dogged, nor destroy all happiness; and yet there was an old saying that when poverty comes in at the door love flies out at the window, which posed her for a minute or two, as it unpleasantly crossed her mind, and made her feel uncomfortable, for she was trying very hard to think her old mercenary views had been wrong and mistaken. The General had interrupted her interview with Mr. St. George, and she had not given him a decisive answer. She had not said " No " positively, and now she was glad of it; but she was not sorry that she had not said " Yes " either. She was, in a measure, free still—pretty much as she had stood before this eventful day—except that she felt sure of what was only a surmise till now—sure that the only person whose admiration and love she ever really valued was serious in his regard for her.

The afternoon was grey and cold, and perhaps depressing in its influence. It was getting more so as the shadows of evening fell, insomuch that Dora felt nervous and afraid as she approached her home. She had often felt slightly nervous under similar circumstances before, because her father possessed such an uncertain temper that she never could be sure of what sort of a reception she would meet with after being out; but her nervousness was of a different kind now. Her heart sank and her hand trembled as she laid it on the gate of Evergreen. It was with the utmost dismay that she beheld her father walking up and down in front of the house. For a moment the idea struck her that she would pass the gate, and not go in just at present. Could her father be waiting for her—waiting to hear the result of her walk with the barrack-master? While she hesitated as to whether she should enter the gate or walk a little further on the road, Captain Bouverie espied her figure in the dusky light, and came slowly down to meet her.

"Well my dear?" he said, as she walked towards him.

"Well papa," she said, trying to speak carelessly, though she found it hard to speak at all.

"Have you had a pleasant walk, my love?"

"Not particularly; I executed the commissions you gave me. I hope they are all right."

Her father put his hand on her shoulder, and looked into her face, but she did not meet his eye. A great many unpleasant feelings oppressed her; but, perhaps, the uppermost one amongst them was that of being ashamed of her father — ashamed of his affectionate way of addressing her now, so different from what it used to be; yet he looked so ill and careworn that her heart smote her for entertaining any thought of him that was not kind and respectful.

"And have you nothing particular to tell me, dear?" he asked, putting his arm round her waist.

"No papa; nothing."

"You mean that you will not tell me anything?"

"There is nothing for me to tell. You

know I walked to Norham, and I neither saw nor heard any one or anything very strange. I paid a visit to Mrs. Skinner, and found her half dead of rheumatism."

" Pshaw !" said the father, growing impatient. " You know very well, Dora, I do not allude to such trifles as that. I want to know what Mr. Clarke said to you during the walk."

" Oh ! he said a great many things; he talks sometimes a great deal, and I do not always listen to him."

" Did he say he admired you very much, and had spoken to me on the subject?" asked the Captain, coming to the point at once rather sternly.

" He said something about it," said Dora, who felt getting quite confused and giddy, insomuch that she had to take her father's arm for support; " but there was an agreement between us that the subject would not be alluded to again till I could give a decisive answer."

" Very well, my dear ; of course your wishes shall be attended to. You will make up your mind quickly I know. I think you already understand what my wishes are."

"I believe I do, papa," said Dora, feeling miserably like a coward— far more cowardly than she thought she could ever be; but it was chiefly because she did not like to startle or annoy her father by an abrupt avowal of her own sentiments, which she knew differed so much from his. It will be easy for some who read this to think or say that she ought to have been straightforward, and declared her opinions and intentions at once openly; but it is not so light a matter to be straightforward always, as might be supposed. Many people fail in this respect, from a dislike of saying what is disagreeable, without first reflecting on the best way to break an unpleasant piece of information. Although in general thoughtless, and even selfish, Dora Bouverie was not so unnatural as to feel indifferent to her father's anxieties and troubles. Hers was a very imperfect nature, indeed; but she was not monstrous. Her conduct had never been guided strictly by principle, but rather by whatever feelings reigned uppermost in her heart.

Like a great many young women, she was very imperfectly educated. Since she was

thirteen or fourteen she had ceased to learn
what her mother could teach her, and she had
not her sister's love of study or reading to induce her to follow up her course of self-in-
struction.   She seldom read even novels.
People who are greatly absorbed by self
rarely care for reading the adventures of
heroes and heroines in fiction.   They have
no sympathy to expend on anyone or anything save themselves.   You will find among
inveterate readers of fiction a greater number
of thoughtful, serious people than you will
find of the light or frivolous kind.   Shy persons, who pass a quiet existence, mixing little
with the gaiety of the world, like to read
novels, and glean from them some little insight into a life that they would not lead for
any consideration themselves.   On a general
principle you will observe that the readers and
lovers of fiction are by no means the most
shallow-brained mortals of the world.   A
very silly man or woman will rarely be induced to read works of either light or heavy
literature.   Some of the most foolish people I
know detest and despise and condemn novels,
and several of the best and wisest whom I

have been acquainted with of both sexes have
been readers of fiction since earliest youth.

" And now, my dear, can you say when you
will let me know what your decision will be
respecting this agreeable proposal, so advantageous in every way? " said Captain
Bouverie, speaking with either real or affected
buoyancy of tone.

"No, papa, I could not ; you know it is
a very solemn thing to decide upon. The
happiness of my whole life may depend upon
such a decision. I must have time to reflect."

" You will take a week, probably, for
this ? "

" Oh ! longer than that."

" A fortnight, then? You must surely
know what your answer will be by that
time."

" Yes; well, perhaps a fortnight."

And, being now close to the house, Dora
flitted through the open door, and ran upstairs.

A fortnight—fourteen days of respite ! It
seemed a good while. Much had happened
within the last fortnight, and much might
happen in the next.

Dora found a letter on her dressing-table
from Ellinor, containing these words—

" MY DEAREST DORA,

"Lady Halesby desires me to say she
would like you to join us here for a week or so,
as we are about to have some company at the
Park.   Gerard—I do not call him Gerard to
his face now, though he sometimes calls me
Ellinor, just as he used to do when we were
children—has asked some gentlemen down to
shoot or hunt, and there may be some ladies
coming also.   You had better get your blue
silk altered and trimmed fashionably, and I
think you will require a new evening dress.
Be as economical as you can, for I am afraid
papa cannot well afford to pay for anything at
present.   Lady Halesby wished to put off any
gaiety here till Dawson should come home,
but it seems Gerard asked his friends some
time ago, and they must come at the time appointed.   Probably Dawson may arrive before
the party breaks up.

"I trust mamma may not be lonely with
both of us away from her.   If she has any
objection to being left by herself, I shall go

home and let you come here, as you would
enjoy gaiety more than I should.

" With best love to all,

" Believe me,

" Your affectionate sister,

" ELLINOR BOUVERIE."

Dora pressed her sister's letter to her lips
before laying it down after reading it.

" Dear Ellinor, you do not know what a sad
heart I have," she thought, as she looked at
herself in the glass, and took off her hat,
wondering that her face betrayed so little the
agitation she had so lately gone through. She
looked pale and weary, but nothing more;
she had often looked the same way for no
particular reason.

" Perhaps I have no feeling like other
people," she thought. " Anyone else would
scarcely be able to endure what I must bear.
If I go to Halesby I shall not tell Ellinor anything about what occurred to-day. I wonder
who will be there. Ah, I don't much care,
unless somebody in particular is among the
guests; yet I may as well go, and forget myself and my troubles, if I can. Something

might happen to cheer us and extricate us from difficulties. I will have hope."

Alas! how often have people hoped in vain! How often do the threatening clouds grow blacker instead of clearing away! There are certain turning points in our lives that seem to lead to dark passages of interminable length, and perhaps the Bouveries were coming to this turning point now.

CHAPTER IX.

REBECCA HAMMOND'S STORY BEGUN.

IT will be remembered that Ellinor Bouverie
had made up her mind to see and speak alone
with the young woman, Rebecca Hammond,
at the Halesby gate lodge. She felt it to be
her duty to do so, though she shrank from it.
Had she not promised to seek the girl again,
it is probable that her heart would have failed
her, and she might never have put her intentions into execution; but having promised
she would not now break her word. The
following morning, before Lady Halesby was
out of her room, and when she felt that it was
not likely she should be missed from the
house, she walked out early through the
grounds, and then went towards the north
gate lodge. It was another dull, calm day,
not bright or cheering. The branches of the
leafless trees were scarcely stirred by the still

air; the sky was of one uniform dim colour,
and here and there a solitary blackbird could
be seen hopping about with lonely aspect. It
was very peaceful, but very dull; yet as
Ellinor walked along she felt as she used to do
in old times, when she was a child at Halesby,
finding happiness and something to interest
her in almost everything out of doors.

Arriving at the gate lodge she found
Rebecca Hammond occupied, as on the day
before, with needlework, given her to do by
Lady Halesby. She was a little surprised to
see Miss Bouverie so early, but Ellinor ex-
plained that she thought that hour would be
the most convenient for her to see her for a
little time uninterruptedly.

" I feel that I can trust 'you perfectly, Miss
Bouverie," she said, " though at first when I
saw you I did not think you could pity
me ; you looked very coldly at me ; and
besides that, I fancied I saw a likeness to a
person who has caused me much misery ; but
then my brain sometimes grows confused, and
perhaps I do not see as others do.   Just now,
I believe you are to be my good angel, and I
will confide in you fully."

Ellinor then said she was ready to listen to

whatever she might have to tell her, and at
Rebecca's suggestion, Miss Bouverie and she
went out of the lodge, and walked together to
a quiet part of the grounds, where there were
some rustic seats, and where no interruption
to their conversation was likely to occur; and
there, after some hesitation, the girl began her
story in words something, if not altogether,
like the following :—

"I lost my father and mother in early
childhood, and my only brother and I were
placed under the care of an uncle who treated
us both very cruelly. My uncle James was a
wealthy farmer, not married, and of very
miserly habits ; he grudged us what we
ate, and clothed us wretchedly. I believe my
father had lent him a great deal of money,
and he had promised to repay it to his children, and treat them with kindness till they
were grown up and able to work for themselves; but he did not fulfil this promise.
He made a farm-labourer of my brother,
preventing him learning anything more
than he was taught at twelve years
old, in our father's lifetime, and treat-
ting him far worse than a common labourer,
for he gave him no wages, and expected him

to be at work late and early. I spent a very
lonely childhood. I had no sister, and though
my brother was good enough, yet I found he
did not sympathise as much with me as I did
with him. One day, when I was about thirteen, my uncle said to me, 'Rebecca, you are
getting a fine lass, and couldn't you help in
the dairywork? I'm thinking of sending
away one of the maids, and putting you in
her place.' I got very angry, and said I
would never be a servant. 'And what will
you be?' asked my uncle, 'for you cannot
expect to be idle here, eating and drinking
up my substance and earning nothing.' I
said that if he would let me go to school for
a year or two, I should learn hard, and try
to become something higher than what he intended me to be; but he laughed at me, and
said that I should learn nothing useful at
school; that it would be all money thrown
away to educate me; and that I should get
ridiculous notions above my station. In some
respects Uncle James was less hard upon me
than on my brother, and by great coaxing
and persuasion I induced him to let me go to
a respectable school near London, where another girl in our neighbourhood was edu-

cated. He bought me a few clothes, gave
me a little pocket money, and said he hoped
I should not have my head turned with folly.
I was very ambitious, and I had heard that
my mother was a high born lady, who was
glad to marry my father, because she had
been obliged to become a governess through
poverty. I determined to be a governess
myself; and at school I got on so well that,
after the first half year, the mistress lowered
her terms, which pleased my uncle, and made
me teach the junior classes. By these means
I was able to remain at the school till I had
learned a great deal, and was fitted to teac h
young ladies the usual amount of accomplish-
ments. I seldom went home to my uncle's
house, even at vacation time. The more I
saw of neatness and comfort elsewhere, the
less I felt happy or contented at the farm.
My brother and I did not write often to each
other; he disliked writing, and when he
would not answer my letters I stopped sending him any. The chief thing I disliked at
the farm, as I grew up, was the familiarity of
the young farmers in the neighbourhood. I
looked down upon them, and thought them
boorish and ignorant. One or two of them

asked my uncle for my hand in marriage, but
I refused them indignantly; and as my uncle
feared he might have to give me some money
as a marriage portion, he did not press me to
accept any proposal.   At last I went away
to be a governess in a family living in London.   The gentleman of the house was an old
acquaintance of my uncle, and he and his
wife agreed to give me what they thought a
liberal salary.   I had three pupils, the eldest
of whom was only eleven years old.   I was
treated here with much kindness and attention, and taken a good deal into the confidence
of the family.   About this time my brother,
getting impatient of his life at my uncle's
farm, ran away and enlisted in a dragoon
regiment, and my uncle was consequently
much enraged at what he chose to call his
ingratitude and disobedience.   He extended
this anger to me, and told me that I need
never expect to receive any countenance from
him in future; so being of hasty temper I
wrote to him to say that I did not wish for
his favour any further, and was quite able
now to earn my bread, and had become independent of him for the future.   Of course
I took my brother's part, though I was

ashamed of him for enlisting as a common soldier. He came to see me once or twice in London, but he soon went to Ireland with his regiment and I did not see him again. I have not seen him since, nor do I know where he is now. I suppose I shall never see him again in this world; I could not bear to meet him."

Ceasing to speak for a few minutes, the young woman covered her face with her hands, and seemed too much agitated to go on with her narration.

Ellinor was greatly interested in her story, but she knew that its worst part was yet to come. She did not break the pause that ensued by saying anything. She was glad to observe that Rebecca was by no means devoid of natural feeling, notwithstanding her stony aspect occasionally.

"The gentleman whose daughters I was educating," continued the girl, "was a very wealthy man. He was a stockbroker, and he had an office in the city; but he and his family lived in a large house in a handsome private street. I was a very good accountant, and sometimes he gave me accounts to make up and letters of business to write. I under-

stood a great deal of his transactions, and was
so much trusted that I was often sent to get
considerable sums of money at the bank
where his money was lodged.   His wife
treated me with greater consideration than
people generally show towards a hired governess.   I often wondered what the use of having a great deal of money was to Mr. Kettleby,
for he did not appear to enjoy himself more
than if he had been a person of moderate income.   He was at his office every day, from
ten o'clock till five in the evening, and even
at home he often spent hours at night looking
over accounts.   I could not bring myself to
value money merely for its own sake.   I
valued the things that can only be procured
by money, but not the mere accumulation of
gold to be heaped up in banks, and stowed
away from human sight.   Yet I used to hear
people say of some shabby-looking creature,
'Such-and-such a man has a hundred thousand pounds, and you would not believe he
was worth sixpence.'   And then everybody
would look with wonder and respect at the
rich old man, shuffling along in garments
nearly threadbare, and with a face furrowed
with wrinkles of care.   I often laughed to

myself at the idea of people thinking the mere
possession of money such an enviable distinction; but the time came, unfortunately, at
last, when I thought nothing on earth so precious as gold, when I should have given my
heart's blood—if it were possible by such
means—to procure a certain sum of money."

Here Rebecca ceased to speak, and became
so pale that Ellinor felt alarmed lest she
might faint.

"I wish I could write the rest of my sad
story," said the girl, clasping her hands together. "I can hardly bear to tell it any
further by word of mouth."

"You are tired now," replied Ellinor.
"Take a little rest, and then you may be
able to proceed. I think writing would
be almost more fatiguing for you than speaking."

Summoning up all her strength of mind,
Rebecca endeavoured to continue her story.

"One summer, in the month of July, Mr.
Kettleby's family went to the seaside, and it
was delightful to us all to get out of town.
You who live a great deal in the country cannot understand the intense pleasure of leaving hot, dusty streets, and going far off to

where the breeze blows freshly, and you can
have the sky clear and broad overhead, and
the atmosphere uncontaminated by unhealthy
vapours.   We went to the small, retired
watering-place of Pentley, a spot you have
not probably heard of, scarcely more than a
fishing village, but with lovely sands, and
neat little bathing lodges.   Oh! how we enjoyed ourselves.   The children and I took
such long walks, climbing over rocks, and
wandering all day and evening by the sea-
shore.   Mrs. Kettleby did not go out much,
or walk far.   The children, as usual, were
left entirely to me.   It was altogether a holi-
day time.   No lessons, no needlework, no
books of any kind; nothing to do but to
scramble over the shingles, or sit upon the
rocks, listening to the plash of the waves, or
watching the fishes leaping in shiny circles to
the top of the water.   It was very lovely, and
very lonely, too; and sometimes, when I sat
in the evenings hearing the incessant murmur
of the ocean, some sad, inexpressibly dreary
thoughts would oppress me respecting the
great mystery of life, and the still greater mystery of death and eternity.

"One evening my pupils and I had wandered a long way on the beach. The weather was warm and calm, and we walked out upon the rocks far from the shore, as the tide was out, and the children wished to look for crabs and seaweed. While they were amusing themselves with their search, I at length sat down to rest, and as usual, fell into one of my fits of musing, forgetting that the time was passing and the evening was closing in. The first thing that roused me up was being startled by finding my feet soaked through with water, and then I saw that the tide was coming in rapidly ; and each minute the rock I sat upon was being encircled higher and higher by the water. In the greatest alarm I started up, and looked for my young pupils. who were much farther from the shore even than I was, and to my utter dismay, I observed that several of the smaller rocks, which I remembered to have seen plainly a short time before, were now invisible. The tide had completely covered them. Even by making the greatest haste in returning to the shore, it would scarcely be possible, I thought, for the children to get back 'in safety. I could see them stooping down, still searching for shells or seaweed, perfectly unconscious of their danger, and too far off for me to hope they would hear me if I called to them. Every moment the rocks that formed a sort of bridge from the spot where I stood, to where they were, seemed growing less and less visible, till some disappeared altogether before my eyes, and the water closed over them, leaving gaps here and there that made me shudder and grow cold with terror. Never before had I felt the power of the sea so forcibly as then. I knew not whether I should go to the children and try to rescue them, or stay where I was and perish. Summoning up all my strength, I shouted loudly to them, and waved my handkerchief, but they did not see or hear. In the space of a few minutes, I pictured to myself the agony of the mother and father when they should learn the dreadful fate of their three children confided to my care. I did not think of myself, though my own peril was almost as great as that of my pupils, and every moment was making it greater. Here and there some high rock, that had been surrounded in the early part of the evening by several lesser, now stood like a solitary speck above the waters. I shall never forget my feelings of terror as I gazed

upon the changing scene before me—changing almost imperceptibly, yet still steadily.

"The eldest of the girls at length turned
her head towards me, and saw my gesticula-
tions and signals to return. She was now
aware of her dangerous position, and she and
her sisters stood looking at me, evidently at
a loss to know what to do. They stood upon
one of the highest points of rock, which had
as yet not been engulphed, and I had a spark
of hope that it might escape the water, at
least for some time; but how to rescue the
children from it I could not imagine, for the
passage from my position to theirs was
gradually becoming a mere waste of sea.
Even if the tide never rose at that time of
the year to such a height as I dreaded, still it
would be a fearful thing to have to wait out
for hours in the night till the waters receded,
for as it was, my pupils could not attempt to
advance on foot to the shore, nor could I at
that time reach them.

" Perplexed and bewildered, with the soft
murmur of the ocean ringing in my ears, and
the air growing damp and cool, I clasped my
hands and resigned myself to whatever fate
had in store for me. I had motioned to the

children to remain were they were, and, indeed, their own sense warned them to do so.
They stood together, holding each other's hands,
and apparently saying nothing. I had my eyes
fixed upon them with such intensity of gaze that
they seemed to sway backwards and forwards,
and the whole sea appeared in agitation. I
dreaded that I should faint, and so lose any
power of helping the poor children, when
suddenly I heard voices shouting, and a little
boat passed within a few yards of where I
stood.

" It contained two men—one like a fisherman, the other a young man, having the aspect
of a gentleman, who wore a sailor's hat, and
a careless, but becoming costume, suitable
for the sea-side. The boat seemed to me to
be sent by Providence.

" ' Do you know, ma'am, that the tide will
soon be full in ?' asked the fisherman, shouting to me, energetically; 'and that rock
you're standing on will be nearly covered by
the water in ten minutes.'

" ' I know it,' said I; 'and there are three
children in still greater danger than I am—
farther from the shore. Can you possibly
save them?'

" The man stood up in the boat, the sail of
which he was about to alter, and looked towards the rock I pointed to.

" ' They'll be safe enough there for a longer
time than you would be where you are,' replied he. ' I don't think the tide can touch
them where they are, but they would have to
wait till near to-morrow to get to shore.'

" ' And can nothing be done to get them
off that rock?' I asked. ' I will promise any
reward if you will only bring them to shore
this evening.'

" ' Nay, nay; we don't want money for
such work as that,' said the man, smiling.
' The difficulty is—if the thing can be done
at all.'

" ' Make haste, for heaven's sake,' I exclaimed, hardly knowing what I said, ' and
try if it be possible.'

" ' The water's pretty high to be sure,' observed the man; ' but the boat might run
aground near those rocks, or if anything like
a breeze came up we would be sure to drift
into the breakers beyond, and so get out to
sea.'

" The gentleman, whom I thought very
handsome, now got up and looked about

him, and said it would be necessary for me
to leave my perilous position at once, adding that they would bring the boat as near to
me as was possible, and endeavour to get me
into it.

" With much difficulty I succeeded in
reaching the boat, having been obliged to
wade for a considerable way through the
water; but the boatman, who knew the coast
perfectly, guided me in safety, and at last,
weary and drenched, and trembling with
anxiety for the fate of my pupils, I found
myself in the little vessel, with the stars
coming out over the sky, and the moon already
rising.

" The tide being quite against us and very
powerful, it took a long time to get to the
spot where my pupils were. Sometimes we
seemed to be making no way at all—in fact
going back instead of forwards. The gentleman, as well as the boatman, used the oars in
turn, and appeared to exert their strength to
the utmost, for it seemed that a part of the
water was very dangerous, owing to particular currents and breakers which rendered it
necessary to go by a circuitous way, causing
much delay.

" Perhaps I have lingered over this adventure longer than was necessary," said Rebecca, as she paused in the narration of her story for a little time; " but it was a very momentous one to me, as it was the commencement of all my serious troubles.

" The children were rescued with much difficulty, and even danger, by the boatman, who behaved with the greatest kindness and courage. The gentleman who accompanied him assisted, of course, and he seemed to understand a good deal about the management of the boat; but still the success of the undertaking was chiefly due to the exertions of the poorer man. It was very late when we got back to the shore, and my pupils and myself were chilled and almost benumbed with cold. I promised the boatman a large reward for his trouble, forgetting in my excitement that probably Mr. and Mrs. Kettleby might not be so well inclined to part with their money on account of an adventure that was caused by my own negligence. I expressed my obligations to the gentleman for his kindness also, and felt inexpressibly delighted when he said he was more than rewarded by receiving my thanks.

He made some other complimentary speeches, also, and said that as he had come to spend a week or two at Pentley, for a little fishing and shooting, he hoped he might see me again. He told me his name, but from what I know now, I think he did not give his right one. I shall call him Dormer, for convenience sake at present.

" Mrs. Kettleby was very angry when I returned that evening, bringing my pupils in, all wet and cold, at about half-past ten o'clock. She had been greatly alarmed at our long absence, and messengers had been despatched in all directions to search for us along the beach, of course unsuccessfully. Nobody dreamed that the little boat out on the water at that late hour contained the children and myself, and some people suggested that we might have been washed off the rocks by the tide. There are some persons who always grow unreasonable, and extremely cross when nervous and frightened. Mrs. Kettleby happened to be one of these people, and she scolded me, for the first time since I came to live with her, saying humiliating things which my temper could not tamely bear. I scarcely deigned to excuse my conduct, but listened

to her words with contempt, saying very little,
but that little was of a bitter nature, and made
ill-will between us almost for ever after ; for
though I, on my part, was sorry for what I
said, yet she did not regret one sentence she
addressed to me on that occasion. In general,
she was not a person easily roused in temper,
and therefore she did not quickly forget her
anger. My life, after that, would have been
dreary and sad in the extreme, only for my
new acquaintance, Mr. Dormer, whom I met
nearly every day or evening, as I walked out
with my pupils—these latter not mentioning
him to their mother, ex cept in a casual way
now and then, as some one who had gathered
particular shells for them, or brought them
sea-gulls.

" Before the time of our leaving Pentley to
return to London, my new friend had spoken
openly to me of admiration, and even of love ;
and as he was the most elegant, and evidently
the best-born person I had ever associated
with on terms that I chose to think equal, I
felt delighted and flattered at first, and full
of bright hopes. My whole life seemed
changed by the wand of a fairy. No one, or
nothing could annoy me now ; Mrs. Kettleby's

cold looks and rude speeches fell powerless
upon me. I was altogether absorbed in my
new dream of happiness, and gradually I
ceased to think of myself so much as I thought
of my lover. At first my vanity and my pride
were flattered by his attentions, but at length
my heart was won completely, so that I considered him perfection, and trusted him im-
plicitly. He told me that he was in the army,
and that he had not much money—that he
had a very unkind father, who grudged him
a sufficient allowance for his requirements,
though he lived more economically than any
other officer in his regiment, and that it was
half for the sake of saving he came to Pentley,
instead of going to a fashionable watering
place. I pitied him very much, and would
have given worlds to be a rich heiress for his
sake. He said his family were very proud
and disagreeable, and that if he married a
person who had no fortune they would dis-
card him for ever. At the same time he gave
me to understand that his father had plenty
of money, and was only of stingy, grinding
habits. Knowing what a man my uncle
James was, I could sympathise with him in
having such a parent, and to meet a debt that

he mentioned as owing, I begged he would accept from me a small sum of money which I had laid by during the last year. He seemed greatly touched at this offer, and though he declined it with a great many thanks at first, yet in a day or two after he asked me to lend it to him, saying he would pay me as soon as his next month's pay was due, or before that day, if he heard from his 'old governor,' as he called his father, a personage whom I had already began to think very unfavourably of."

"I am afraid he was not a good young man," said Ellinor, with a kindling eye. "He would never have spoken of his father and his family in that way, if he had been. No matter what a father or a mother may be, I think a child ought never to allude to their faults before strangers. I fear I should have considered this Mr. Dormer an extremely mean-spirited person."

"But, remember I was in love, Miss Bouverie—the most passionate, unreflecting stage of love—when nothing of that sort could make me turn against my lover. You have probably never been in love yourself yet, or

you would know how much is forgiven and
passed over under such circumstances."

"I am perfectly sure I should never love
an unworthy person," said Ellinor, colouring
slightly.

"Not if you knew him to be unworthy
before you loved him," returned Rebecca.
" But first, love, and then you will see no
fault afterwards, except perhaps some dreadful fault impossible to be overlooked, some
unmistakably evil conduct. I was glad to be
able to assist my lover, and proud that he
accepted the money I offered to him. I never
wanted it back, and I told him so, but he
asked me if I believed him capable of such
dastardly conduct as to deprive me of my
earnings longer than a few weeks, and seemed
so mortified that I said no more on the subject. The time for our departure from Pentley
was now near at hand, and I looked back
upon my stay there as the happiest period of
my life, indeed perhaps the only happy period
I could recollect, for I could not bring back
any pleasant remembrance of my starved and
miserable childhood at my uncle's farm.

"Mr. Dormer promised to write to me

when he left Pentley, and he did so. I considered that first letter the most precious of precious letters. It contained nothing very striking or decisive, but it assured me he would love me always, and remember our happy walks over the sands as the brightest spots in his life. I carried that letter with me everywhere, till its edges got worn and frayed, and then I laid it by to preserve it. Of course I had told my lover all about Mr. Kettleby's position, and where he and his family lived in London, and it was agreed between us that we were to meet there. I considered that Mr. Dormer was only delaying a regular proposal of marriage from fear of his unkind and tyrannical father. Once or twice he threw out hints about a secret marriage, but I objected to it. I said I was satisfied to wait, and that if he would remain true to me I should ask nothing further at present."

CHAPTER X.

THE TEMPTER AND THE TEMPTED.

" We met as we had promised, in London,
and he told me that his circumstances were
more embarrassed than ever. He appeared
in the greatest distress at not being able to
pay back the money he owed me; and even
said that he had unavoidably become plunged
into still greater difficulties, adding that he
had been inveigled into giving security for a
friend, for whose insolvency he had become
responsible; and in short that his perplexities were innumerable. I believed every word
of what he told me, and felt most miserable,
not on account of my own few paltry pounds,
which I had lent him. but for his difficulties
and the cruelty of his family.

" We had long conversations together, during our walks in retired places. He said he
often was afraid of being arrested, and even

hinted that he might lose his commission if something were not done for him. What could I do to help him? Yet still he used to talk as if it were in my power to contrive something towards his relief. At last I said,

" ' Oh! I wish that I could assist you. I would almost give my life to save you from these worrying cares !'

" ' You might probably assist me,' he replied, ' and it would not be such a difficult matter either. It might be in your power to procure some money for me as a loan.'

" ' How ?' said I, in surprise. ' There is no one who could, or who would lend me even ten pounds in the whole world; I have quarrelled with my uncle, and my poor brother is far away, with scarcely enough of money to meet his own wants.'

" ' Is not Mr. Kettleby a very wealthy man ?' he asked, looking at me steadily.

" ' Yes; but he is a great miser. He would not lend anybody a shilling. I often heard him say so ; besides he is not in London at present.'

" ' Where is he ?' asked Mr. Dormer.

" I replied that he had gone some time ago to Paris on business; and then Mr. Dormer

seemed plunged in thought. This was about
the beginning of winter or late in the autumn,
after our return from the seaside.

"'Do you love me really, Rebecca?' he
asked, fixing his eyes on my face with a
terrible look. 'Do you really mean me to believe that you would give your life to spare
me agony and disgrace?'

"'I mean it thoroughly,' I replied; 'but
unfortunately my life or death could not avail
you anything. If I killed myself here on
the spot, what good could come of it?'

"'None, indeed; but by living and acting
you might save me. Surely you would not
refuse to risk a little on my behalf?'

"'No; I would risk anything for you, but
the loss of honour and my good name,' I
said.

"'And yet there have been women who
have risked that much for one they loved,'
he replied, rather bitterly. 'I am afraid
your regard for me is colder than I believed.'

"I felt very much offended with him for
saying this, and for a few minutes even some
doubts of his worthiness filled my heart. I
scarcely dared to think of what he wished

me to do. He had never presumed to wound me directly by any insulting speech, though sometimes he had thrown out hints of how happy people might be who gave up the whole world for each other, and cast aside all the trammels and formalities of society ; but though I now think he meant nothing honourable by such remarks, I did not then understand their tendency. After his expressing doubts about my really loving him I grew annoyed, and reproached him for being unreasonable and unjust, and he told me he was only in despair.

" ' You say you do not value your own life,' he observed, ' and most likely you do not value mine either. Perhaps it may not cause you any great emotion to learn that I have a fixed idea of putting an end to my existence if I cannot discover some means of becoming relieved of my embarrassment.'

" ' If there were any way on earth that I could devise, I would do it,' said I, in agony.

" ' There is a way,' he said, ' and though it seem a desperate one, it is in reality easy enough.'

" And then he disclosed to me a plan of meeting his bills, which would fall due before he could possibly get money from his father.

"I can hardly bear to disclose the dishonourable and iniquitous proposal he made to me. I blush for human nature as I recall it, and yet, infatuated as I was, I still pitied and trusted him, even after he had made such a request of me. He knew that I was often employed by Mr. Kettleby to write letters for him and to make up accounts, and sometimes to fill up cheques for him, all to the signature. I had told him that I could copy any handwriting shown to me after very little practice, little dreaming that he would ever take advantage of this information; but to my dismay he now proposed that I should prepare a false cheque for a large sum of money, and, signing it in Mr. Kettleby's name in favour of his wife, get one of the clerks in the office to have it cashed at the bank where the stockbroker's money was lodged, and so secure the amount unknown to anyone. At first I was shocked at such a proposal, and declared that it would be utterly out of the question for me to comply with it. I said the Kettlebys had been kind to me, and I could not betray their confidence; and then

he declared that the Kettlebys need never be
at the slightest loss, or even become aware of
the transaction, as he would certainly have
the money to pay back into Mr. Kettleby's
name in a few days, or at most a week. My
own sense told me that whether the money
was paid into the bank or not, the cheque
drawn by me in favour of Mrs. Kettleby
would remain in all probability to confound
me at some future time ; yet, still there might
be confusion about it, and as long as the bank
accounts were not sent to Mr. Kettleby, and
if no more money were actually missing, the
transaction might possibly escape notice. My
lover's distraction, or apparent distraction,
his declarations that he would take his own
life, unless relief arrived for him, and my
own dreary conviction that the world possessed
no tie for me but this one all-absorbing love,
which was my sole hope and stay on earth,
induced me to lend my hand to the committal
of a base fraud—a crime that in former days
was punished by death.

"One winter night I got Mr. Kettleby's
cheque-book where I knew he kept it, and
after some hours in copying and re-copying
his hand-writing on slips of paper, and in

thinking of the awful step I was about to take for the sake of a person whom I had never heard of a few months ago, I at length accomplished that dark deed. I knew very well I was doing wrong. I knew it as well as I know it now. I did it with my eyes open, my understanding unclouded; but I was doing it for another—not for myself. I was doing it for a person dearer to me than my own life, and whose misery was worse than death to me. I know not whether I can be excused in your eyes, Miss Bouverie, or in any eyes; I fear I cannot. That love, or blind passion, which carries us away from a sense of duty and gratitude, cannot be regarded as a worthy feeling. I think myself, now, that I was under a delusion of Satan. From the hour that I wrote and signed that false cheque I felt that I was a lost creature, steeped in crime; and when I finally sent it to the head clerk in Mr. Kettleby's office, with a note purporting to come from Mrs. Kettleby, for whom I frequently wrote letters, my excitement was beyond expression. Filled with dread and anxiety, I watched all day for the arrival of the clerk or his message with the money, that I might intercept it, and was obliged to feign illness in order to account for looking so badly, and for remaining indoors all day.

" After the office hours the clerk came, and the money was left for Mrs. Kettleby in a sealed envelope ; as she happened to be driving out with the children, I opened the envelope and found the sum correct. The figures on the notes seemed to waver and flicker before my eyes, yet with a strange infatuation I went on looking at them over and over again, till my brain grew perfectly confused, and I kept repeating the numbers of the notes with a fearful bewilderment. Mr. Dormer came that evening, and I handed him the money, saying that I had now sacrificed for him as much as he could expect from the most devoted love. Yet even then I felt that the capability of loving him, or anything on earth, seemed to grow faint within me. My heart appeared suddenly to become changed and hardened. I was unable to say much to him, and his assurances that he would immediately replace that large sum at the bank, gave me neither comfort nor hope. I had committed a crime that could not be blotted out by any common reparation. In my own conscience I must always suffer; my self-respect could not return, or buoy me up as it did of old. I felt like a thief and a robber, full of duplicity and meanness. I considered myself a felon."

"And the man who was the instigator of the crime?" asked Ellinor, as her brow flushed and her eye brightened—"the man who was more than an accomplice, and who acted by far the baser part in the transaction—what did you think of him?"

"I was too much absorbed at first in a sense of my own degradation to think much of the part he had played. I felt that I had been doomed to a sacrifice that I could not escape from, but which would darken my whole future life. For several nights I did not sleep, and I felt often as if my brain could scarcely bear the weight that pressed upon it; yet I had to try to keep up during the day-time, and teach my pupils, and listen to their childish prattle, feeling all the time like the description given by Hood of Eugene Aram, as he sat apart from the merry boys that came bounding out of school.

"Thank God, I was not a murderer. I had not taken human life; but I had broken faith and wronged those who had trusted me. My brother and I had always abhorred dishonour; my uncle had abhorred it too. Our family had all been remarkable for upright principles. I was to be from henceforth a black sheep and an outcast. I had not withstood temptation. I had disgraced my name, and I could not expect to feel upon an equality with my own brother any longer. Even supposing that my crime was never to be discovered, I could not presume to hold up my head, and feel the same freedom of spirit I had felt of old; I could not be a hypocrite to myself, and cheat my own heart with flattering delusions.

" I wrote to Mr. Dormer, imploring him to say what he intended to do, to save my employers from feeling that they were robbed, and declaring that I could not endure the torture of mind I was suffering. His answer was the last stroke given to my agonised spirit. I received a most insulting letter, saying that he pitied me from his heart, and that he was enduring great pain for my sake; but that he found it perfectly impossible to refund the money at the time appointed —in fact, perhaps for several months, he

might not be able to do so. He then went
on to say that if I were afraid to remain at
the Kettlebys, I could find a refuge under his
protection, where no one would either know
him or me.

" I tore that letter across, from top to
bottom, and would have mangled it into
shreds, only a sudden idea of revenge possessed me, all at once, and I determined to
keep it, torn as it was. I should not have
been so enraged about the money, had he
said nothing to insult me ; but in an instant,
as it were, after reading the letter, my eyes
seemed opened to his perfidy and his dishonourable principles. I thought that another
monster of iniquity scarcely existed on the
earth. He had made me his dupe from first
to last. Whatever sentiment he had felt for
me, it was not the love I had believed in and
hoped for. I was humbled and wretched—
yet fiery in my wrath. Revenge was to be
my watch-word now. I vowed on my knees
that he should be brought to open shame, if
I had to travel ever so far to accomplish my
purpose. To stay at the Kettleby's I could
not dare, even had I wished to do so. Every
day brought terror to my heart after Mr.

Kettleby's return. When I beheld him making up accounts, or when he addressed a word
to me, I felt my heart stop beating. Mrs.
Kettleby, too, began to throw out hints about
my being negligent of my pupils, and of
certain rumours that prevailed about my being
seen in company with a strange gentleman,
who seemed to be of too high rank to associate
with me for any creditable purpose. This
galled and enraged me. He of too high rank
to be my equal! The beggar on the street
was not less of a gentleman than he was!
One day among some of my papers I met
with a piece of a letter, which had been
written to my perfidious enemy (I will no
longer call him my lover). I remembered
that I had picked it up one day after he had
lit his pipe with part of it; and I had kept
the fragment of paper because I thought the
handwriting very pretty, and also on account
of its being a portion of a letter written to him,
for at that time every trifle connected with
him had a charm for me. This piece of a
letter, as I now saw, curiously enough revealed to me, among the few words left of it,
the name of a place where he was expected
to be at a certain time. I prepared to leave

I 5

the Kettlebys either secretly or openly, but surely. To my uncle I could not dare to go, even if we had had no quarrel. I knew not where my brother was, for I had not heard rom him for months, and to tell the truth I had always felt ashamed of him since he enlisted. Alas! how much more was I ashamed of myself now. I had, therefore, no friend on earth to fly for refuge to, even had I wished for one. Henceforth I felt that I was to be a wanderer until my resolution was fulfilled; and after that there would always be death by which to end my sufferings.

"I bought a suit of clothes at a shop where second-hand garments were sold, and kept them in readiness for my departure from Mr. Kettleby's at any time. This suit that I wear now is the same. I thought I should look less remarkable in it than in better materials and brighter colours. I had scarcely any money; there was some due to me in Mr. Kettleby's hands, but I would not ask for it, even if I were to starve for want of means. I daresay I was a little—perhaps, a good deal crazed; I thought I looked so.

"One evening Mr. Kettleby asked his wife, in my presence, what money had been drawn

by her during his absence from the office, and
I felt as if a blow had fallen on my head; one
side of it feels numb since.   She said she did
not remember that she drew any; she thought
not; and then he said no more on the subject.   Perhaps it was a mere chance question
without meaning, for Mrs. Kettleby could
always get money in her husband's absence
from the cashier, at his office, whenever she
required any.   But still a great terror seized
me, and I prepared to leave the house next
morning.   I wrote a few words on a sheet of
paper, and left them on my dressing-table,
running thus:—" I am going away because I
have wronged you; I was tempted and
wronged myself; but if you have no com-
passion for me, have some for my brother and
my uncle.   I will do what I can to repair the
injury I have done if you will wait for a
little time."   I then signed my initials and
left the house.

"It was a dark, most dreary morning in
December, not yet daylight, but the clock told
me it was time to be on my way. I took only
a small bundle of a few things, among which
were the letters my perfidious enemy had
written to me, and his picture which he had

given to me. I was now going in pursuit of him. The few words of the torn letter which I have already mentioned told me the place he was expected to go to about Christmas— that place was Norham, which, I have since learned, is a great military garrison. Towards Norham, then, I directed my journey, filled with the idea that I should soon discover him. Want of money kept me long on the way. Sometimes I walked as many as twenty miles in a day, and sometimes, when nearly ex-hausted, I travelled by railway for some dis-tance. You know how far Norham is from London; yet I should have walked the whole way, only I found the effort impossible. When my money was drawing to a close I was obliged to go on foot, and I was near the end of the journey when I arrived at the village of Lidcombe in a dreadfully weary state; here I took the train as far as Halesby, and on reaching that town, tried to walk to Norham, but I sank in a fainting state at the gate-lodge of Halesby Park, and have since been unable to pursue my travels. The kindness of Lady Halesby has been very great; and I was carefully tended through a long, feverish illness. It is now past Christmas, and I know

not whether my enemy may have left Norham;
but I shall trace him even so; I feel certain
I shall yet stand face to face with him, and
denounce him before all people as a swindler
and a robber. You know he was dishonourable and criminal; you cannot blame me for
wishing for revenge."

" I consider him to be one of the worst
type of criminals," said Ellinor, earnestly ;
"but you must let me tell Lady Halesby your
whole story. Miserable and sad, as it is, it
might even yet be worse, and I think it is
best that your benefactress should learn the
exact truth. She will advise you how to act,
and her influence is great; she will know
whether Mr. Kettleby should be informed of
the manner in which he was defrauded; for,
unless he takes some steps in the matter, he
will certainly lose the money drawn at the
bank by the forged cheque. The young man
who tempted you to act in such a way should
undoubtedly be found out, and, if possible,
be made to refund the money, and he ought
to be punished heavily."

" But *I* should be tried for the forgery !"
said Rebecca, shuddering. " My God ! I
could not bear such disgrace for my brother;

I would die first. Perhaps you have a brother of your own, Miss Bouverie, and you may understand how you would shrink from dishonouring him—how much you would suffer rather than let a blot rest upon his name."

"I will tell the whole story to Lady Halesby," said Ellinor, pressing her forehead with her hand; "and believe me, I pity you from my heart. The man capable of taking such mean advantage of your interest in him is below censure—he is monstrous!"

And then she went away towards the house.

CHAPTER XI.

LADY HALESBY'S VIEWS CONCERNING A
DAUGHTER-IN-LAW.

As she had intimated to the unhappy girl,
Ellinor considered it her duty to repeat all
that had been confided to her to Lady Halesby,
whose mature judgment would assist them
in coming to some decision as to what course
should be pursued. The length of time which
had elapsed since Rebecca left Mr. Kettleby's
house, and the non-appearance of any notice
in the public papers respecting the forgery,
seemed to show that it had either not yet
been discovered by Mr. Kettleby, or that he
did not intend to prosecute the culprit. There
had not been any reward offered for her apprehension ; as yet there was nothing but her
own conscience to alarm her in her quiet
retreat at Halesby.

Without any delay Ellinor sought out Lady

Halesby, and gave a short, but concise version of the sad tale, and the latter listened attentively, expressing occasionally great horror of the young man Dormer, whose iniquity Ellinor particularly and emphatically dwelt upon, in order to point out the great temptation the girl had received to sacrifice her own truth and honesty, and become plunged in crime, in order to prevent him committing suicide.

"You see, my dear," said Lady Halesby, " we cannot be certain that the man Dormer was anything but a thorough swindler from first to last; it is most likely he never was in the army at all, and that his poor victim was deceived respecting him in every way. I have no doubt that the account she gives of herself is correct; she seems a very truthful person, and certainly she has tried to place herself in a creditable light. She has displayed great weakness of mind, to say the least of her crime."

" Yes, and I suppose the man who led her into it, understood her character when he dared to propose anything so dishonourable to her."

"This uncle of hers, of whom you tell me

will be the proper person to communicate
with respecting the young woman," continued
Lady Halesby, "and we must find out the
real names of all parties concerned. I could
not undertake to recommend a person of her
character for any responsible position ; and,
therefore, her own relatives will be the only
people likely to afford her protection and
shelter when she leaves this. As to her
betrayer, it is not probable that we shall ever
hear of him; most likely he is in America, or
on his way to Australia by this time."

"But she said she discovered that he was
to be at Norham about Christmas."

"That looks as if he belonged to some
branch of the Military Service, for Norham is
not a place where strangers can come without attracting notice. It could afford no
shelter for a criminal."

"No ; and for that reason I fear he may
be some wretched, unprincipled young man,
quartered, perhaps, at Norham, at the present
moment. How dreadful to think of it!" said
Ellinor.

"Yes, shocking, my dear; God help his
family, if he has one! Yet, I should say his
parents may blame themselves for his

depravity. I always think the dishonour of
a child reflects sad disgrace on his natural
guardians. Depend upon it, no well-brought-
up youth ever turns out unprincipled. There
must have been great want of religious and
moral teaching, where people come to a bad,
disgraceful end. Several young men of the
present day (and, indeed, it was too much the
same in past days) are allowed to grow up
with very lax ideas on all subjects connected
with religion and morality. They smoke,
and drink, and run into debt, considering it
quite a manly act to keep a tailor or boot-
maker out of his money for an indefinite
period, perhaps for ever ; and people scarcely
blame them unless they commit some extremely criminal act. We hear a great deal
about the training of girls, as the future wives
of England ; but few people consider the
training to be given to the husbands of those
young women. The happiness of men is
taken into great account, and provision made
for their domestic comfort; but the happiness
of women must be very lightly regarded when
we find so little real solicitude to provide
virtuous and pious husbands. A young man
might be very spirited, and by no means

deficient in those qualities which are termed manly, though religious and leading a blameless life. The bravest men are, and have been, the best Christians; the greatest cowards have been generally both cruel and depraved in every respect. It is not altogether a mother's partiality, Ellinor, that makes me believe my own son to be a very highly-principled young man. I have the greatest confidence in his good sense and religious feelings, and I only trust that when he thinks of marrying, he may meet with a wife as good as he is himself—a wife who possesses a thorough sense of honour and duty, not a merely amiable namby-pamby woman of undefined character; but a really worthy, energetic, high-minded person, who will be able to guide and assist him in all noble works. He has very good abilities himself, and much discernment and sound sense—gifts often more useful in our every-day life than more glittering attributes; yet, I should like him to marry a woman of high talent and intellect—not the so-called high intellect, which some very silly persons of both sexes are said to possess, but that large grasp of mind and reason which makes the owner

almost God-like ; that deep understanding
which enables the possessor to comprehend
what is great, and what is small, and to
sympathise with the weakness, as well
as with the noblest thoughts of human
kind. So far, my dear Ellinor, from thinking
that people who have much intellect are
heartless, or that strength of brain and
tenderness of feeling are incompatible, I
believe that the most highly intellectual and
deeply-reasoning men and women are also
the kindest and most benevolent. Never run
into the error of thinking that foolish people
are good-natured. On a general principle
silliness and selfishness go hand-in-hand
together, just as cunning exists with a low
order of intellectual capacity. Yes, dear
Ellinor, I should be glad, indeed, to see my
son the husband of a truthful, honourable
woman, who came of unblemished, well-prin-
cipled family, without blot or stain—a woman
of strong mind, and kind heart, and who was
not vain or worldly; above all, I should like
her to love him for himself, because I think
in marriage it is more important to the
happiness of both husband and wife, that the
wife should love deeply, even where the hus-

band may not altogether do so. I have
known several instances in families of miserable disunion, all owing to the fact that so
many women marry men they are indifferent
to, and whose affection they never learn to
prize, or to return. How wretched 1
should be were Gerard doomed to such a
fate !"

" You require a great deal, I am afraid,
in your idea of a wife for him," said
Ellinor, blushing a little, as Lady Halesby
turned round and looked at her.

" No, my dear, I do not; I only ask for
mental qualities of a high order. Beauty of
person, of course, is all very well, too; and I
value it as something lovely to look at; but
I do not consider it indispensable as a quali-
fication in a daughter-in-law. Good birth I
prize highly, but I do not want fortune for
my son. Having no brothers or sisters, he
will have a far larger income than his father
married upon. If he loves a good woman,
who is worthy of him, and who really returns
his love, 1 shall be only too happy to consent
to his marrying her, as soon as they both like.
His father entertains ideas on this subject
very like my own. Don't you hope that

Gerard may be happy in his married life ?"

Ellinor could only answer, " Yes," very faintly ; and to her great dismay she knew that her face was growing more and more flushed, as Lady Halesby took her hand, and pressing it in her own, looked again full at her.

Could Lady Halesby have discovered that her son entertained more than a mere cousinly regard for her? And knowing it, could she countenance and wish to promote it? Could such happiness really be in store for her ? It was too much to believe ; thoughts of such a possibility forced themselves into Ellinor's hand, bewildering and overwhelming her, making her ashamed of her great presumption in imagining for a moment that she could reach up to the high standard of excellence required by Lady Halesby, in her ideal of a daughter-in-law.

CHAPTER XII.

SIR RALPH BARNARD IS CONCERNED FOR THE

SAFETY OF HIS AIDE-DE-CAMP.

AT Evergreen Villa, Dora Bouverie was making a few arrangements for her visit to Halesby, not with the lightness of heart she might have felt under the same circumstances a month ago, but merely as a sort of duty.

She was too busy trying to alter her own gowns, and making sad mistakes in the process too—for she was by no means an expert needle-woman—to get out to walk much at this time, and she did not see anything further of Mr. St. George for some days. Once or twice, when she went out on business, she did not meet him, and she scarcely regretted it, for she felt in a very vague, uncertain state of mind. There were no invitations to the Bouveries for any parties at this time at Norham, though parties were

given pretty often in the town and in the immediate neighbourhood.   Mrs Skinner was
giving dreary little soirees to bring Mr Dozyhead to a regular proposal for her elder
daughter; and so he attended them in a
semi-sober state of intellect, once being so
much off his guard that he informed Miss
Skinner she looked astonishingly well, considering her years; and that it was " a confounded length of time" since he first fell in
love with her; but Miss Skinner did not pretend to hear him; she only looked more
vinegary than usual, determining probably to
have revenge at some future period.

Miss Barnard gave parties also, and was
sorely disappointed at the results.   Mr.
Gerard Lyon happening to be pre-engaged
always latterly when he was invited to the
General's; but no one who went to those
parties knew how little she valued his or her
company, for she wore the same stereotyped
smile and soft expression of countenance as
usual, and just said exactly what was right
and proper with her wonted agreeable stupidity; and the poor deluded mortals still
said, " What a nice girl she is !" and went
home satisfied with her, but very dull, feeling

an unaccountable dejection of spirits, and as
if evening parties, after all, were scarcely
worth the trouble of dressing for.

Mr. St. George did not make his appearance
in the vicinity of Evergreen, owing to the
fact that the General kept him pretty close to
himself all this time. Indeed Sir Ralph was
beginning to think he should send Mrs. St.
George a letter stating his apprehensions
with respect to her son, and suggesting some
possible means of saving him from a very imprudent marriage. In days when the General's
heart was not so hard as now, he had
been an aide-de-camp himself to Mrs. St.
George's father, and he had fallen in love
with that lady when she was a pretty girl,
into whose company he had been thrown in
one of the West India islands, where the
young lady's father held a military command.
But Sir Ralph was at that time only Mr.
Barnard, a lieutenant in an infantry regiment,
and he did not think himself a fitting match
for the beautiful Laura Ponsonby, who, while
he was hesitating and doubting on the subject, was taken to England by her invalid
mother, whose health the tropical climate did
not suit, and so ended the first love-dream

of the young man. Laura married soon
after her arrival in England, and the match
she made was poor enough in point of money.
She became the wife of the younger son of
Lord Killeeven—the Hon. Frederick St.
George—who was given the living of Gartoquil as the best thing that could be done for
him ; and she subsided into a very useful
rector's. help-mate, respected by the parish-
ioners, and satisfied to live in a remote country
district of the North of Ireland with many
hopes filling her heart, touching a brilliant
future for her handsome son, Rodney. Marrying in after years, and getting a considerable fortune with his wife, Sir Ralph Barnard
found himself at length in a position to bestow patronage on former friends, and having
become acquainted with the son of his old
love, he offered him the appointment he now
held as aide-de-camp, feeling a very paternal
regard for him, and determining to watch
over his interests. There is little doubt that
the young man would have felt more grateful
if the General had pursued a different line of
conduct, and let him, in plain words, mind
his own business ; but Sir Ralph was doing
everything for the best, and his only fear was

that he should find himself defeated at last. That walk down the street of Norham, with the two young people conversing so earnestly, and too absorbed to see him until he was quite near, with the clatter of the horse's hoofs rattling loudly in their ears, filled him with considerable apprehension. He felt that if St. George was not proposing at that time, he was not far from the awful step ; and then he comprehended how futile must be the attempt to check the courtship, by merely keeping the young people asunder at formal evening parties.

" Rodney must leave Norham for a time," he thought, " and he will soon remember this passing fancy as a foolish, a very foolish piece of business. To be sure I was desperately in love at one time myself; but then Laura Ponsonby was a very different person from Dora Bouverie."

Every man thinks the woman he loves, or has loved, very different from any other, the difference being, of course, in her superiority. It is this delusion which makes so little real sympathy exist generally for lovers in their anxieties or difficulties.

If Mr. St. George did not walk so often on

the Evergreen-road, another person, no less
worthy, though perhaps not so striking-look-
ing, might have been and no doubt was, seen,
taking an afternoon or evening stroll on it,
many a time and oft, at this particular season
—which person was Mr. Trydell, the chaplain to the forces, and the quiet lodger of Mr.
and Mrs. Barr, in Church Street.

Latterly Mr. Trydell had got himself into
disrepute at Norham, owing to his conduct
at a meeting assembled there for the purpose
of impressing upon the public mind the disgraceful treatment practised towards the
women of the East by the men of the East.
It so happened that a Deputation from a certain Society in the person of one somewhat
stout, short gentleman, made his appearance
in the town; and collecting a meeting—con-
sisting, of course, almost entirely of the
female sex---then and there gave a very har-
rowing picture of the dependence and of the
slavery of the women of the East.   He was
an enthusiastic and energetic speaker, and he
pointed out in forcible language the great
degradation of the poor creatures whose cause
he was advocating.   He declared that in that
extraordinary part of the world, the East, the

females (he meant the human females) had a
very inferior position to that of the men ;
that females were excluded from society, and
only looked upon as servants for their husbands ; that they got the worst of everything,
and were not considered in any way as on an
equality with the men. That they were
denied education ; they had no rights, no
privileges. That from the time of their birth
to the hour of their death they were slaves.
After causing all the sixty-six eyes of the
thirty-three women present at the meeting to
flash with indignation at the thoughts of the
dreadful men of the East, he caused them all
to glow with admiration as he spoke of the
great contrast which existed in the treatment
bestowed upon the women of England, who
held such a different—such an elevated position. He did not enter into the particular
points of difference that existed between the
respective treatment of the Eastern and
Western women, nor dwell upon any public
rights enjoyed by the females of Great
Britain. In one sweeping outburst of elo-
quence he said the women of England were
highly influential, highly prized, and worthy
of the honour given to them ; he took it upon

him to say that they were happy, and that they had nothing more to wish for than they already possessed. He concluded by saying he hoped all the ladies present would contribute, out of their abundance, towards providing funds for carrying on the work of raising the position of their much despised sisters in the East. Some of the poor old ladies, who were before unconscious of any particular elevation of position, unless that which they possessed in having been obliged to occupy second-floor lodgings since their husband's deaths, now quite plucked up a little spirit, and looked around them triumphantly. It was true that they had not, upon an average, quite forty pounds a year each, and were necessitated to look very shabbily dressed, and to feed very poorly—some of them who could afford to keep servants being obliged to take them out of the workhouse for economy, and to experience great worry of temper in teaching them how to attend upon them. Their limited means since their widowhood commenced had not unnaturally impressed them with the belief that the position of the female sex was less fortunate, nay, considered extremely inferior, even in Great Britain,

to that of the male sex.   Indeed, it almost
appeared to these ladies that the male in-
fants of this country were born with what
is popularly and figuratively termed silver
spoons in their mouths—it was so much easier
to provide for young men than for young
women; and there was often so much poverty
in families, particularly orphan families that
abounded in daughters.   Imagine their pleasure, then, in being informed by the deputation that the women of England were regarded as highly honoured, and that they
wielded great influence, and that they stood
in this fortunate, blessed land, perfectly on an
equality with the men of England.   On the
whole, the greater part of the old ladies were
proud and happy till Mr. Trydell got up in
his turn to speak.

Now Mr. Trydell, while listening to the
deputation's eloquent address concerning the
degrading   treatment   experienced   by   the
women of the East, felt some terrible mis-
givings in his mind, that the picture drawn
by the aforesaid deputation was, in principle,
merely like an exaggeration of what was
going on—ay, even at the present moment in
the West.   It struck Mr. Trydell that there

was a great resemblance between the position of the females of his own country, at the present time, and that of the women of benighted Eastern lands. If the female children in the East were little cared for when born, and in some few instances were let perish as useless little creatures, were there no instances ever known of great disappointment being caused in so-called civilised European nations by the birth of a daughter, instead of a son, because —ay, in the West itself—there are laws expressly made to prevent titles and estates from descending in what is called the female line ? If the women of the East were regarded more in an animal than in an intellectual light, and were excluded from society and debarred from the advantages and pleasures of education, could it be said that there was every facility given for the mental elevation of the women of the West ; that there were Universities endowed liberally by this country for the education of women—nay, could it be even said that women were members of the learned societies of this kingdom, or that they were encouraged in a pursuit of knowledge by a woman ever receiving, or having the faintest hope of receiving, any title or public mark of recognition for any amount of learned research ? If the women of the East were kept in the background, where were the women of the West kept ? If ladies in this country cannot really dare to break through the absurd bondage of the escort system, and must necessarily meet with insult even if it became the fashion to dispense with attendance at public places, then we must only deplore that our country is still but half civilized, and its men in a semi-barbarous state. Men ought to be ashamed if it is through fear of meeting with insult and rudeness from them that women are shut out from so many places both of amusement and instruction, and that their lives are thereby often rendered very dreary and monotonous. How many clubs and reading-rooms there are in our cities and small towns, where the men of all ranks, from the peer to the humble mechanic, may sit and read books and papers for hours, and yet how few similar facilities are afforded to women for the enlightenment of their understanding. Where are the reading-rooms for the women of the lower orders ? Even a literary gentlewoman may find it a difficult matter to secure a sight of the notices and reviews of her own works, unless her publisher be obliging enough to forward them to her. A lady going into a public reading-room to look for literary reviews among the newspapers or magazines would create as much surprise in any of our cities as if she walked out in Turkey without a yash-mac over her face ; and yet she will find very few of her nearest male relatives either able or willing to look out for these important notices on her behalf, and to give her a correct report or a correct copy of any one of them. Men are generally busy about their own affairs, and are not always very bright-witted. It requires a very quick eye to scan, in a few moments, the contents of a newspaper, and to find out speedily the particular portion one is looking for; and there are not many men who will take the disinterested trouble of examin-ing, day after day, dozens of papers in search of something that may or may not be there, for the purpose of obliging a friend. The maxim of doing a thing yourself if you want it to be well done, is, no doubt, a very wise one ; and if women could do for themselves a great deal of what is generally deputed to be   done   for   them   by   their   male friends, it is certain that they would fare all the better for it. Could any one affirm that there was a general disposition among the men of Great Britain at even the present time to extend any rights to the women of the country greater than those which they possessed of old, at the time when serfdom and puerile superstition reigned in the land?

Mr. Trydell could not help himself from thinking on this wise. It was true, he thought, that English women were not obliged to have their faces uncomfortably covered up from the public gaze, nor were they excluded from attending balls or parties of pleasure, provided the unmarried women had qualified persons to take charge of them on the flatter· ing supposition that they were unable to take care of themselves—but were they not excluded from every public position that could bring them substantial honours or rewards? They had no voice in the senate of their country; and up to the present moment they, though obliged to pay taxes, were denied the right of voting for members of Parliament. Except in some disgraceful, or disagreeable case, connected with insult, wrong, robbery—

crime of some sort—a woman's name rarely appeared in public. It did not seem to Mr. Trydell that his countrywomen held either a high or independent position. Latterly owing to Mrs. Barr's conversations respecting her views of female education and training his attention had been drawn to this subject, and he had considered it a good deal, which caused him to feel rather confounded when his turn came to speak at that meeting in expected condemnation and contempt of the manners and customs of the Musselmans and Hindoos. He could scarcely help believing that every one in the room must think as he did ; that the eyes of the whole assembly must be open to the true state of the case, as it appeared to him, and that they would con-sider it hypocrisy for him to chime in with the common cant. Filled with these ideas he commenced his address, by observing that notwithstanding the similitude that unhappily existed still between many of the customs which prevailed respecting the women of the East and the women of the West, he yet trusted that advancing civilisation would in process of time blot out from all lands every trace of that spirit, whose origin was sin,

which had influenced men in all ages and in
all countries in their treatment of the other
sex, up to the present time ; and Mr. Trydell
was proceeding to point out what he thought
should be reformed in this respect in his own
country, when he suddenly found himself
assailed by fierce looks from many of the
elderly ladies, who had been so charmed to
hear how influential the deputation had considered them ; and likewise by the deputation himself, who turned round in wonder to
gaze at him as he spoke ; insomuch that Mr.
Trydell grew confused, and was unable to
proceed.   A fit of coughing fortunately came
to his aid, and for a few minutes he was not
called upon to utter speech, but it was vain
for him to try to recover any popularity for
that evening.   He had insinuated that the
women of England were not influential, and
had no independence ; and that here they
stood very far indeed from being on an equality
with the men.   He had sent the poor old
gentlewomen flying back to their former position of inferiority, with no hope to cheer them
of living to see any more civilised age coming
in their time ; and they resented his words
bitterly.   They would not submit calmly to

the degradation; they did not believe in it.
How could Mr. Trydell, who had lived so long
at Norham, know as much about anything as
a deputation, who very likely came from
London, and whose face they had never seen
before? The ladies flashed all this at poor
Mr. Trydell out of their indignant eyes, and
he bungled henceforward in what he wished
to say, and concluded his address abruptly,
having offended the deputation who expected
to be supported in his condemnation of
Eastern customs, and having called down upon
himself the ill favour of many of the assembly. It was in that way he got into the disrepute we have alluded to. The ladies talked
next day of his extraordinary sentiments, and
the low opinion he entertained of the women
of England; and some of them had serious
intentions of abandoning the church where
he preached, and betaking themselves to some
other place of worship, but they were obliged
to resign the idea on reflecting that the sittings in the military chapel where Mr. Trydell
officiated were free, and that in the more
fashionable church at Norham they had to be
paid for; and though they were independent
gentlewomen of England, they had not enough

of money since their widowhood to spare for
church sittings; therefore they must continue
to form part of Mr. Trydell's congregation,
whether they liked it or not, unless they chose
to abandon public worship altogether.

One forgiving old lady sent the chaplain
some black currant jelly for his cough, which
seemed so dreadful at the meeting, but as it
had not returned after that occasion, Mr.
Trydell won an unbounded amount of confidence and affection from little Linny Barr, by
presenting her with the kind offering as the
best use he could make of it.

I have said that he was frequently to be
seen walking on the road to Evergreen; and
sometimes when he had passed the villa and
climbed the hill that lay southwards, he
would stand a long time looking down at the
pretty house, with its ornamental chimneys,
and picturesque windows, lying in the hollow,
surrounded by trees and shrubs of never-
failing verdure, while a sad feeling of hope-
lessness and desolation would steal over him
as he gazed.

CHAPTER XIII.

SOMETHING ABOUT THE BARRS AND MR. CLARKE.

ABRAHAM BARR felt more and more inclined, as time wore on, to take gloomy and cynical views of life and human nature; simultaneously with the entertainment of which views he became more and more inclined to neglect his work and disappoint important customers, so that Mrs. Barr grew uneasy, and found it necessary to lecture and remonstrate, and occasionally to coax him to fulfil the promises he had made, and earn the money she expected for the support of the family. If Mrs. Barr did not approve of women working for their own maintenance and independence, she was extremely rigid in her ideas of what men ought to do for their wives and children —looking, as she did, upon husbands and fathers as sorts of machines, to be set a-going

for the benefit and support of their families,
and forgetting that the machines were liable
to get out of order and break down and
sometimes (indeed pretty often) to die out
altogether and cease from working for ever,
leaving the helpless wives and children in a
very unpleasant predicament—the widows,
let them be as stout and hearty as might be,
and as clear of sense and intellect as possible,
being often obliged to fall back upon the
grudging charity of near relations, or the doubtful benevolence of the public.

Mrs. Barr certainly expended a great deal
of energy in trying to get Barr to do his duty
as bread-winner of the family. She was
obliged to soothe violent customers who came
wrathfully from the barracks to make
inquiries respecting furniture ordered weeks
before, and solemnly promised to be dispatched
forthwith to them without delay; worse than
all, she was necessitated to tell small fibs in
excusing her husband's delinquencies—such
as letting it be understood that Barr had not
been very well lately, when in truth he was
suffering from no ailment whatever. It was
positively dreadful, and Mrs. Barr herself
felt inclined to become irritable and distrustful

of human nature, and to bestow less pains
than formerly upon Mr. Trydell's breakfasts
and dinners, and not to care particularly
whether he were comfortable or the reverse.
Owing to Barr's laziness this winter she could
not buy a new gown for herself, nor new
clothes for her children; and the family
dinners had to be somewhat lessened in
quantity and deteriorated in quality; and the
boys grumbled—wishing they were tall
enough to enlist, whenever their mother tried
to set homely fare before them, while Lucy
would sit listening to the grumbling and the
discontented conversation of her mother and
father and brothers, with a strange carelessness as to what was going on around her,
and a somewhat vacant look, as if she were
gazing at something very far off indeed.

All Lucy's bright colour was gone away at
this time, and a good deal of the brilliant
light in her eyes had died out too, and it
seemed as if there were some great fear upon
her—some haunting anxiety that she could
not battle with or overcome, hanging round
her and keeping her from attending to her
usual every-day duties.

Mrs. Barr was glad that her daughter had

given up her evening walks, and her running out of doors at unseasonable hours to speak with friends who kept standing outside the house and would not come in; but still she was annoyed at her for acting very much like her father, and disappointing several customers who gave orders for needlework and found her unpunctual in the execution of it. Then, when the postman was coming round in mornings and evenings Lucy irritated her mother by running out always in such haste to watch for him. It could not be possible that she had taken a fancy to him—"a common fellow like that"—and there was nothing particular or remarkable that ever came, except the payment of a bill at times few and far between. Alas! indeed, poor Lucy's watching of the postman was very vain at this time—vain, but still persisted in with a beating heart day after day, and evening after evening.

In my opinion, if any man has a right to walk with a strut of dignity, and to knock at doors with a summons of exceeding importance, and to pull door-bells with an imposing violence, it is the postman. I never see a postman without feeling a certain interest in him, and something of solemnity, as I gaze at his leather bag, containing so many messages of sadness or of rejoicing—such strange, varied missives, each of which may hold so much within a little compass. Who can listen unmoved to the quick step of the postman running up to his or her hall-door, or to the loud, peculiarly-timed two knocks he gives for admittance? Who has not felt a dull blank as he or she, watching for the postman, sees him relentlessly pass by without stopping? Day after day, and evening after evening, Lucy Barr felt this blank, as the postman either passed by her father's house, or only brought letters for others. There were none for her, and each time that she was disappointed she felt hopeless for about an hour; at the end of which period she would begin to pluck up courage again, and to think the next time the postman came round he would bring her what she wished for.

Thomas Hammersley had never written to her since he left Norham on furlough; she had heard nothing of him since they had separated that bleak, wintry evening, when the snow fell and the wind blew so drearily.

Had she been too proud that night in not asking him to send her a letter? Had he been annoyed with her for anything she had said or not said? Had he found his sister in affluence and grandeur, among gentlefolk, and would he be influenced by her, and never care for her any more? It was very perplexing, and Lucy blamed herself chiefly in the matter.

This state of anxiety and unhappiness went on for several days, and at last a rumour reached Miss Barr's ears which turned her anxiety into actual terror. Military servants and sergeants dropping in at the upholsterer's upon business and for gossip, said that a fine young fellow in the Lancers had deserted lately, having got a few days' furlough to go to London, and having never been heard of since by any one at his regiment. Nobody cared to ask or mention his name.

Abraham Barr only felt interested in sergeants, and knew nothing of privates, or even corporals, and he merely said "Humph!" and that he never thought much of the Lancers. If her life had depended upon it, Lucy could not have summoned up courage to ask

the name of the supposed deserter, though
what could have seemed a more natural
question? Some days elapsed before she was
certain that his name was Hammersley; but
she became certain of it at last, and her heart
died within her. Had her lover dishonour-
ably escaped from his military bonds, and fled
to distant lands? Had he been telling her
falsehoods respecting his position and his
prospects, and was he merely an adventurer,
without name or character? To think ill of
him; then, to think well of him again, and to
grieve and forgive him, was what Lucy did
at this time alternately; but there was a
dreadful horror haunting her lest he might be
pursued and captured, and shot.

About this time, Mr. Clarke, the barrack-
master, used frequently to come to the uphol-
sterers to ascertain the price of different articles of furniture, and to make bargains touching the exchange of certain chairs and tables
which he wished to part with in lieu of others
more new and fashionable. Although considered to be wealthy, the barrack-master was
griping and penurious, and fond of grinding
down any one with whom he had dealings,
more for the purpose of annoying and getting

the better of the people from whom he was
purchasing the goods than merely from any
feeling of wishing to economise on his own
behalf.

No one was too humble for Allan Clarke
to hope to triumph over him ; and whoever
dared to thwart him generally felt his power
very severely.   He would pursue any individual, who seriously offended him, with the
most persevering efforts to obtain vengeance.
He was a man of very active mind, not above
the consideration of the smallest matters, yet
capable of comprehending very deep questions, too ; a person of peculiar capacity and
temperament—ever on the watch, scarcely ever
in repose, and determined to attain any object
he had in view, however difficult it might seem
to be to gain it.

Latterly, he had fixed a discerning eye
upon Abraham Barr, and he watched him
steadily, and was watching him still.   For
some months he had ·entertained doubts as to
the upholsterer's good opinion of himself, and
his willingness to submit to him, and cringe
to him, and bear whatever he chose to lay
upon him ; and, therefore, when he was fre-
quenting the Barrs' house at this time, making

bargains, and asking the cabinet-maker to do
what was really beyond his power, he kept a
very watchful eye upon him, and was noting
down in his memory every surly expression
of Barr's sinister face, and every gruff answer
from Barr's mouth, and every flash of scorn
from Barr's differently-coloured eyes, with the
keenness of a hawk, and the patient scenting
of a detective.

Although as much in love as it was possible
for him to be, the barrack-master was by no
means altogether absorbed in this love, to the
exclusion of other common-place feelings.
Even when he had not as much hope of suc-
ceeding in his aspirations as he had at present,
he never felt so utterly bewildered and
dejected as to lose sight of saving or making
money, or of any opportunity afforded him of
annoying sundry of his fellow-creatures.
Perhaps his very attachment to Dora
Bouverie originated from the instinct he
might have possessed that she did not like
him, and from a desire to overcome difficulties.

Now, when he felt nearly as certain of
winning her—indeed, of having already won
her—for his affianced wife, as he was of his

own existence, he went steadily about his usual duties, and was even making preparations for the reception of his bride in her new home. He was satisfied with the matrimonial bargain he was about to make, though Dora Bouverie had no fortune, because he knew the advantages and disadvantages on both sides were pretty evenly balanced. She was young, beautiful, and penniless; he was twice her age, not handsome, and, though of respectable birth, was not particularly elevated in rank, but of sufficient means to maintain her more comfortably than he knew she was maintained in her own father's home. With his detective spirit he had found out exactly the sort of life the Bouveries led at Evergreen, and how sadly the two daughters of the family were neglected by their father. He was the most, in fact the only, intimate friend Captain Bouverie possessed; and he knew better, perhaps, than anyone else, the precise state of his finances, and the likelihood that existed of a crash coming which would make it well for at least one daughter to escape in time to some other refuge than that which her present home could long afford her. Yet, in spite of these apparently cool calculations on the subject of his marriage, it must not be imagined that Mr. Clarke's love for Dora Bouverie was a faint one. Had he been a man of less energy and activity of mind, it might have overwhelmed his other thoughts and feelings, and have interfered extensively with sober duties ; but he was a person capable of being interested in a great many things at once, and one who never allowed himself to neglect necessary business in his eagerness to pursue any favourite scheme. A steady man he seemed, yet not a wise one, as you will hereafter find out. There are many plodding, persevering people by no means sensible—very many crafty individuals who, after a long continuance of successful plotting and manœuvring, find themselves outwitted in the end.

Now, it so happened that the barrack-master considered that Abraham Barr should work for him on a much cheaper scale than for other people, because he had the power of patronising him, and bringing him into notice with military men when they arrived at Norham, and also because it greatly depended on his influence whether the upholsterer were permitted to leave furniture in the barracks after certain customers there had left it, till it was convenient to have it removed from the rooms. In many ways, of course, Mr. Clarke had a great deal in his power, and he liked to let it be known how influential he was. In some instances he actually wanted Barr to work for him, and upholster chairs and sofas, without receiving payment at all, and the cabinet-maker agreed to do so several times, feeling that if he made an enemy of him it would be a bad thing for himself and his family; but somehow or other Abraham was getting fractious of late, and a spirit of rebellion was rising within him. It might take some time yet to burst out, but burst out it would, sooner or later. He was determined that he would not stand such tyranny and oppression very much longer.

There was scarcely anything that Mrs. Barr dreaded so much as the sight of Mr. Clarke coming down the street, or stopping at her door to give orders for furniture. Not that she grudged him her husband's gratuitous labour, for she thought it better for Barr to be employed, even if he were to get no pecuniary reward for his work, than to be idly wandering about, picking up gossip, or spending money at shows and such vain amusements, but she felt a most unpleasant sort of presentiment that Abraham would declare war with the barrack-master ; that there should be an open rupture, and all their comfort at an end. Generally she used to try to be present at any interviews which took place between Mr. Clarke and her husband, that she might soften down whatever either might say that was unpleasant to the other; but it was a hard thing for her to have to stand between them, and listen to the sharp commands of the one and the moody replies of the other, feeling all the time that it would take a very little sentence to overthrow all semblance of respect and consideration on the part of Abraham.

One afternoon the barrack-master came to the cabinet-maker's house and asked to see Barr, who was forthwith summoned from his workshop, where he was reading a newspaper, for he liked to be *au fait* of all the political news of the day.

As ill luck would have it, Mrs. Barr happened to be out doing a little shopping upon this day, and was, therefore, unable to interpose her influence as mediator between the

hostile parties.   Abraham was not in particularly good humour, and he rather resented
being called away from his paper.

"I want a lounger covered with the best
damask," said Mr. Clarke, when Barr appeared before him. He scarcely ever deigned
to preface his orders by any civil salutation,
or inquiry after the upholsterer's health, but
entered at once on his business in his sharp,
peculiar manner. "It must be the very best
damask."

"And of course the very best price," said
Barr, with a sinister glitter in his eyes.

"That it will be the very highest price, if
left to yourself, I have no doubt," responded
the barrack-master, with a slight sneer.

"I'm so griping, I suppose, and so mean
and so untruthful," added Barr, grasping the
back of a *prie dieu* chair that stood near him,
with one large, brown, bony hand, and
looking very straight into the barrack-master's
face.

"The lounger must be ready by to-morrow
week," said Mr. Clarke, not pretending to
observe the sinister expression of the upholsterer's face, yet observing it very closely all
the time, and making a note of it to add to the

store already in his memory. " I require it
punctually for that time."

" And about the payment of the bill that's
due already ?" returned Barr, unflinchingly,
still looking straight at his superior with a
half contemptuous, whole doubting look.

" That bill you had no right to send to
me," answered Clarke, coolly. " It is an im-
position. I gave you to understand that I
should not pay for such trifles as that. You
should have understood that I don't consider
myself bound to do so. You owe me a great
deal more than I ask from you. A word of
mine and you would lose the patronage of
the garrison in a week; not an officer at
Norham but would get his furniture elsewhere. You know very well that this is not
the only upholstering establishment in the
town."

" And could a gentleman think of taking
the bread out of a tradesman's mouth for a
paltry bit of spite ?" demanded Barr, with a
dark flash coming into his strange eyes,
that made them both appear, for once in his
life, of exactly the same colour.

The brow of the barrack-master slightly
lowered, but a half smile played about his

mouth, giving his countenance a most unpleasant expression. It would have been difficult to determine which of the men looked the more repulsive at that moment.

" Do you intend to obey my orders or not ?" asked Mr. Clarke.

" Do you intend to pay my bill?" asked Barr, quivering with passion.

" Certainly not," replied the barrack-master.

" Then I refuse to work for you any more," returned the upholsterer, in a voice husky and agitated. War was declared at last.

" You mean to say that you defy me in this way?" asked Mr. Clarke, still maintaining perfect control over his temper; "you mean to say that you openly refuse to obey my commands?"

" I spoke plainly, and I meant what I said," replied Barr, doggedly.

" And you make up your mind to bear the consequences of your impertinence and ingratitude, of course?" continued Clarke.

" I am not afraid of any ill consequences from what I have said or refused to do," said Abraham, now standing erect; " I am a free

man, and my word is as good as the word of
the highest in the land.   I can speak and tell
my story, and the public will listen to me.
We don't live in a country, thank God, where
there's a different law for the rich and the
poor."

Clarke smiled, and there was a glimpse of
triumph in the smile.

"You are a fool, Barr!" he said.

"I daresay I am.   If I had been as crafty
and as cunning as others, I would never have
done work for any man for nothing.   I should
never have submitted for a moment to be
trampled upon, and cheated out of my lawful
money."

"You will repent yet of the words you
have spoken this day; you will yet be ready
to fling yourself at my feet, and beg for pardon," said the barrack-master.

"I beg for pardon from any man?   I fling
myself at the feet of any being of flesh and
blood like myself?" said Barr, with intense
contempt pictured on his countenance.
"Thank God, I am not so far fallen as that!
No, Mr. Clarke, you have no right to order
and bully me; you have no right to cross
my threshold, and command me to do what I

don't consider just and fair. I am an independent man, not a slave ; I may work for my bread, but so do you, so does everyone nearly in some degree in every rank; yet, as long as we act uprightly, we are entitled to consideration and respect. I should regard myself this day as a dog if I let myself be tyrannised over by you or anybody else !''

" Enough of this sort of balderdash !" said the barrack-master, scornfully. " I understand that you refuse to undertake work for me, and persist in the most extraordinary and impertinent behaviour I have ever witnessed in a person of your class."

" I refuse to work for you without payment, having worked for you long enough, unrewarded and unthanked, even by civil words, empty as they are ; and you may understand anything about my impertinence that pleases you," replied Abraham, who still trembled with excited and indignant feelings.

There could be no retraction now; no going backwards of what had been said or insinuated. Even if his passion permitted him any glimpse of calm reflection, Barr could not fail to perceive that he had launched out

on a hitherto unknown sea, and that having
done so he must prepare himself for all the
consequences of his rashness.

Mr. Clarke did not waste much time in
wrangling or disputing with the upholsterer;
he scarcely seemed to be moved at all by his
independent mode of addressing him; in fact,
one might have thought that he rather tri-
umphed in witnessing this outburst on the
part of Abraham Barr. What he had long
foreseen, and watched for, had come to pass
at last. He could now put forth his powerful
hand and crush the cabinet-maker like a worm.

The barrack-master did not like to hear that
Dora Bouverie was going to Halesby even
for a short visit; he feared to let her out of
his sight; and he was particularly annoyed
because be envied the wealth and rank of the
people who had invited her to their house.
He had never been asked to the Park himself,
and of course he felt inimical to the Halesbys;
but Dora was not in his power as yet, and he
could not presume to interfere with her plans
or wishes. The only thing he could now do
to console himself was to try and find out who
were invited from Norham or eleswhere to

form the guests at Halesby. He was uneasy and anxious upon this subject, and jealous, and rather inclined to malignity. The days were passing, and a week had already elapsed since he had told his love to Dora. In another week he had a right to look forward to her answer. Her father had informed him that she should then put him out of suspense. To do him justice, it must be admitted that Clarke felt inclined to keep his promise of not talking on the subject of his proposal to Captain Bouverie till he should receive Dora's final answer to it from herself; but he was not satisfied with her, and he feared she might prolong her stay at Halesby, and shrink out of coming to any decision respecting her acceptance of his offer till some indefinite period. He did not doubt that she should yet be his wife, but he wanted the matter to be settled formally and speedily.

As to Dora herself, she tried to banish thoughts of his proposal as much as possible. As she had informed Mr. St. George, she had long been accustomed to escape from reflecting on anything that was unpleasant to her— and certainly the idea of marrying the barrack-master was most unpleasant, and, in fact,

odious to her. While making preparations
for going to Halesby she sat nearly always up
in her own room, out of sight of her father and
mother; and, of course, she was lonely and
depressed, feeling that she had nothing hope-
ful or invigorating to cling to. It is a curious
fact that she rarely thought of anything that
did not in some way directly concern herself.
Upon Ellinor's prospects she scarcely ever
dwelt, and it did not occur to her that her
sister might, in all probability, redeem the
fortunes of her family by making a prosperous match. Perhaps it was because Ellinor
was so little accustomed to talk of herself and
her admirers that Dora so seldom thought of
her sister's matrimonial prospects. She could
know very quickly who her own admirers
were, but she was singularly blind to the admiration that Ellinor excited. There is no
doubt that she would, on the whole, have
been much happier if she had thought less of
herself and more of others, and extended her
interests and sympathies generally.

At Halesby Ellinor was making herself
both useful and agreeable to her friends; and
Lady Halesby was keeping upon her a
very steady, scrutinising look-out from her

stony, expressionless eyes, unknown to anybody.   Had there been any sham, or
manœuvring, or underhand trickery about
Miss Bouverie, her acute kinswoman would
have discovered it all in a very short time ;
but happily there was not.   Ellinor went
onwards straightforward and honestly, and
as far as she was concerned herself she had
nothing to fear from the closest watching.

" How was it that Dawson did not come to
spend the Christmas with you, as he used to
do ?" asked Lady Halesby, as she and
Ellinor were sitting together one evening
before the expected guests had arrived at the
Park.

" I really do not know," replied Ellinor,
who had always felt of late an unpleasant
sensation whenever her brother was alluded
to.   " He does not often write home, but I
suppose he was unable to obtain leave at that
time."

" I should like him to be here while we
have our company.   I thought he would have
joined the party.   Gerard and he were always
such companions."

Ellinor was sure that Gerard had never told
his mother how Dawson had borrowed money

from him, and she began to breathe a little
more freely.

" I gave my brother your kind message
when I wrote last," she said; " and I am sure
he will come here in time if he possibly can."

" I do not know what there can be to keep
him. There is nothing so remarkable going
on at Aldershott just now that he could
not be spared. Is he not at Aldershott at
present ?"

" Yes, his regiment is stationed there."
And Ellinor tried to change the conversation
by taking up a newspaper that lay on the table
near her.

" I was reading something of a murder in
one of the papers lately as having occurred
in the neighbourhood of London—at Grimbsy
Common, I think—a mysterious sort of business. Do you remember it ?"

" No; I never read about murders if I can
help it," said Ellinor.

" Oh! I read everything. One must know
what is going on."

Lady Halesby now got up and looked about
for the newspaper in which she had read of
the murder she alluded to, and, after some
searching, discovered it.

" This is the paper, I think. Look over
it, Ellinor, and find out where that murder
is," she said, handing it to her young
friend.

Ellinor did as she requested, and came
upon a paragraph headed " Mysterious Case
of Murder in the Neighbourhood of London,"
which she supposed Lady Halesby wished her
to read out, and she accordingly did so.   It
ran thus:—

" On Friday morning the body of a man
was found lying in a dyke, at Grimbsy Common, bearing evidence of a brutal attack by
some person or persons unknown.   Although
life was not quite extinct when the body was
discovered little hope was entertained of
restoration even to consciousness.   Several
contusions were found upon the head and
face, and other parts of the body, and the
ground in the immediate vicinity of where the
man was discovered bore traces of a struggle,
which leads to the supposition that the victim
of this ruffianly assault must have made considerable resistance to his antagonists before
he succumbed.   He was a young man of
respectable appearance, apparently not more

than five-and-twenty, but so disfigured in face
from the injuries inflicted, that his features
were scarcely distinguishable.   No clue has
as yet been discovered as to who he was or
where he came from.   He was conveyed to
hospital immediately, and has since, we understand, expired.   An inquest will, of course,
be held."

   " These are the sort of crimes that make us
despair of human nature ever becoming re-
generate or truly civilised," said Lady
Halesby, as Ellinor ceased reading.
   " And for that reason I should never regret being ignorant of such things," replied
Miss Bouverie, laying down the newspaper.

CHAPTER XIV.

DORA BOUVERIE WILL NEITHER SAY YES NOR NO.

THE visitors arrived at last at Halesby. Some came at the time appointed; some came later than they were expected; but the latest of all that arrived at the Park was Dora Bouverie. Being one of those people who never measure 'time exactly, and who never calculate how long it may take to accomplish a difficult piece of work, this young lady was generally late upon all occasions; and she was a day and a half behind time at Halesby—having at last packed up the gowns she had been trying to alter, in a very unfinished, useless state, and having written a somewhat desperate order to her dressmaker at Norham to make her two most fashionable dresses, for evening and morning costume, of any material she thought proper, and trim-

med in any way she liked—so as they could
be ready the day after the command was
issued—and despatched with all speed to her
at Halesby Park.

Dora had never asked her sister who were
to be at Halesby, as she felt a little nervous
and anxious on the subject, and feared to ascertain anything dispiriting concerning the
guests. A faint glimmer of hope now and
then found its way into her heart—but it was
very faint indeed. One thing she was sure
of—that Mr. Clarke would not be at the
Park; and there was a great relief in that
certainty. To escape from all possibility of
seeing him, or hearing his loud, jerking ring
at the door-bell, was something to be thankful for.

Instead of arriving at Halesby early, as
expected, on Monday, she did not make her
appearance there until Tuesday, barely in
time for dinner ; and everything was so stately
and grand that she could not send a servant
to the drawing-room, where the guests were
assembled previous to going to the dining-
room, to summon her sister to her; but was
obliged to go straight to her room and dress
herself as quickly as possible, with the aid of

Lady Halesby's maid, who was in high good humour because some gaiety had come at last to the dim old house, after a long interval of dreariness.

It was pleasant to the ears of the pining domestics located in that ancient mansion to hear the grating of so many carriage wheels as had left their traces on the gravelled sweep up to the house within the last two days, and to hear the tramp of feet and the hum of voices sounding through corridors and long deserted rooms; for servants had come as well as their mistresses, and strange valets and ladies' maids were enlivening the inferior regions of the mansion with pleasant chat. It was altogether a pleasant time at Halesby, and even in the neighbouring town shop-keepers seemed to feel an elevation of spirits in telling their customers of all the gay doings anticipated at his lordship's.

Fine clothes, and expensive jewellery, and fashionable manners can do a great deal to-wards enhancing beauty or softening down ugliness, but they cannot make people appear really handsome when they are remarkably the reverse; and, after a time, those persons who see a great deal of such making-up, and

adorning, and careful setting off to advantage
of every little charm, grow tired of that sort
of thing, and begin to look out for real,
downright beauty, which requires no such
puffing up and embellishment. There is no
doubt that Dora Bouverie would have worn
all sorts of expensive garments and decked
herself in costly jewellery if she had possessed
money enough to procure them; but, as it
was, of course she and her sister were obliged
to dress simply, and to wear few ornaments;
and yet their good looks were such that people
might have thought they dressed thus to let
it be seen how little they required from the
assistance of art.

Coming into the drawing-room with only a
faint flush on her cheek to betray that she
felt any particular emotion upon entering a
well-filled room alone, Dora looking so graceful and so beautiful that people unconsciously
paused in their conversation to look at her as
she walked up to Lady Halesby with a half
smiling, half deprecating look that gave her
the aspect of a most winning simplicity and
innocence; and yet, in a moment or two, before her hostess had finished her few sentences

of greeting, and her inquiries for her father and mother, she had ascertained, with the quickness peculiar to her, exactly who the people were that composed the occupants of the room, and the sight of one of those occupants gave her such a thrill of emotion that the faint flush on her cheek grew fainter and died away altogether in a very short space of time. Her sister met her with looks of pride and pleasure, which were not lost upon Lady Halesby or some others in the room, and as the young girls stood together for a few moments there were few who did not admire them.

The person whose appearance in the drawing-room caused Dora such peculiar feelings was Mr. St. George. She had scarcely dared to hope that he might be at Halesby, because she knew Lord Halesby did not often entertain the military at Norham. Indeed there were sad complaints of his unsociability, and Mr. St. George had been only asked to the house because he had been introduced to the family by mutual private friends. When a man has a large fortune he must expect to be abused if he does not expend a goodly portion

of it in providing for the amusement of others.
The garrison at Norham generally felt that
they were rather ill used, because Lord
Halesby preferred the cultivation of turnips
and mangel wurtzel to social intercourse with
his fellow-man, and, consequently, he was
spoken hardly of, and laughed at, and said to
be very mean, because he made up his own
accounts and his own estimates of expenses,
and was supposed to be doing that most
reprehensible thing—accumulating a large
fortune for his heirs and successors. Lady
Halesby was not much liked either, and no
doubt some of the very guests that evening
assembled under her roof, and partaking of
her hospitality, were animadverting in their
own minds upon how she looked, and what
she said or did not say. Although dressed
for company in richer attire than usual, she
looked scarcely less severe than upon ordinary
occasions. She wore a black velvet gown,
unrelieved by a speck of white; a few dia-
monds sparkled on her here and there, as
rings and bracelets, and a brooch; but she
had the air of being very simply attired, and
wore that stern, immovable expression of face

that made most people afraid of her, and think
they would be very sorry, indeed, to incur her
contempt or displeasure.

The only people who had been asked from
Norham to Halesby, besides the Bouveries,
were Mr. St. George and Captain and Mrs.
Carpendale, who happened to be connected
with some people who were connected with
Lord Halesby; and two young officers
quartered in the town, who had in days of
old been school companions of Gerard Lyon.
From more distant regions had arrived Lord
and Lady Kempton (elderly relatives of Lady
Halesby) and their grand-daughter, Lady
Mary Shelbank—a very young girl, only just
"out," and, though youthful and blooming,
by no means so pretty or attractive as might
be imagined; a certain Mr. and Mrs. Vansen
Hopwood—very wealthy people, but an ill-
matched couple, the gentleman being about
twenty-five years the senior of the lady, who
had married him quite of her own accord, but
seemed to regret the step a good deal since
she had taken it, and looked pitiably mournful,
yet resigned, in costly garments, and adorned
with many jewels of great value; besides one
or two persons more not of any particular

note, chiefly sporting young men without much money to give them distinction.

Mr. St. George did not accost Dora Bouverie immediately on her entrance to the drawing-room; yet he had eyes for no one else after she had made her appearance. As in her case with respect to himself, he had not asked her sister previously if she were coming to Halesby, though he had some secret hopes that she might come, and it was only in the general movement that took place before the guests were finally marshalled off to the dining-room that he ventured to approach Dora and say a few words to her. The difficulty that there had seemed of late in their seeing each other even out-of-doors made this half-unexpected meeting at Halesby doubly grateful to both. What happiness to think that many whole days of sojourning under the same roof were before them!

Seeing him standing near her young relative, Lady Halesby asked Mr. St. George to take Dora down to dinner, and thus the measure of their bliss was full. For a long time Rodney made no allusion to their last remarkable meeting, which had been interrupted so miserably by Sir Ralph Barnard; but he knew from the expression of Dora's face that she was not unfavourably disposed towards him. At dinner they did not speak very much, but they were thinking almost entirely of each other, to the exclusion of everybody else. It was a very pleasant evening to most of the company. If Lady Halesby was not particularly animated her husband was, and Gerard Lyon helped to do the honours of his father's house with a very good grace.

After dinner there was music and conversation, and as Dora Bouverie did not pique herself upon her playing or singing, she was glad to be let sit peaceably in a corner, talking again in the drawing-room, as in the dining-room, to Mr. St. George. No one was watching them, for Mrs. Carpendale, who was the only person there that knew anything of the attention which the aide-de-camp's devotion to Miss Dora Bouverie had attracted at Norham, was greatly occupied in executing wonderful pieces on the piano, and in singing airs in several different languages, or in trying to catch the attention of any gentleman near her (except that of her husband, at whom she generally looked scowlingly whenever he approached

her), so that she did not care much who else
was flirting or looking about for admiration.

Before the night was over, Mr. St. George
had ventured to ask Dora if she would not
give him some reason to hope that she had
not forgotten what he had said to her during
their last interview at Norham, and that she
had considered it since then, in a favourable
light for him. But this direct inquiry sent
her back all at once to the remembrance of
that other proposal she had received the same
day to which he alluded, and a shadow came
over her face and over her spirits.

" I cannot give you any decided answer to
that," she said, in a subdued tone. " I feel
very much flattered at your good opinion of
me, but I am not my own mistress. There
are others to consult as well as myself."

" Then give me permission to apply to
Captain Bouverie, " interrupted Mr. St.
George.

" Oh, not for the world !" declared Dora,
hurriedly. " You do not understand; you
cannot understand how I am situated. As
long as I am here I can say nothing decisive
to you. In about ten days I might be able
to give you a definite answer."

" And if you had only your own feelings to consult, might I dare to hope?"

" Perhaps that is scarcely a fair question," said Dora, trying to speak calmly; " yet I think you ought to know—that is, I am sure you might know that if I had no regard for you I could give you a very decided answer on the spot. You must be satisfied to wait for a little time—that is, if you are sure that your regard for me will last up to that period."

" Believe me, my attachment is not of such a fleeting character as you seem to think," he said, earnestly, and with something of reproach in his look and tone.

" At all events, I shall not bind you to any promise, nor shall I bind myself either. I must be free for the whole week that is coming. Sometimes I feel a *presentiment* that this is the last week of happiness I shall ever know !"

Dora smiled faintly as she spoke, but there was a very sad expression in her eyes at the same time. There were people who had told Mr. St. George that she was a coquette, and a heartless, giddy girl, who had no feeling for any one but herself, and even now as he looked at her, and heard her words, which, after all, might merely mean a sort of putting off from coming to any conclusion of an affair that he earnestly wished to be settled, a slight misgiving came over him that she was trifling with him, intending to keep him hanging about her for an indefinite period, but never meaning to accept him finally. He had been informed that she had been often guilty of this sort of vain coquetry in the case of other lovers. Of course, people had exaggerated her enormities in this line, and invented several instances of glaring cruelty on her part, though it was very hard upon her detractors to have to acknowledge that any man ever admired or loved her sufficiently to suffer great misery at her final rejection of him. The way they took to bring her down was by saying that all the suitors she had ever possessed were poor, weak-minded young men, whom she first allured by every species of trickery and deceit, and then cast off in the most shockingly barbarous manner.

"You will not keep me long in suspense, I trust?" said the young man, rather dejectedly.

"It does not depend upon myself, I assure

you," she replied, earnestly. "I shall not be at liberty to speak as if I were my own mistress for a certain length of time—not so very long either."

He did not look at all satisfied; but she was not to be moved from her resolution, and they went on talking on indifferent subjects.

"Ellinor seems very happy, and looks quite pretty," thought Dora, sometimes pausing in her conversation with Mr. St. George, to watch her sister, as she went about among the guests, at Lady Halesby's request, helping to entertain them, and looking animated and bright-eyed. "Shall I tell her how miserably I am situated, and what perplexity I am plunged in?"

No, she would not let her know anything of her troubles for some time at least. She shrank from confiding them even to her sister. Perhaps she knew that she was not without blame herself in the way these troubles had come upon her. She must have been aware that she was not acting in a straightforward manner with any one concerned in them, and it is probable that she feared to ask Ellinor for either sympathy or advice.

How would it all end? But she would not think. She would enjoy the few days that were coming, and leave the time beyond that, to its own revelations.

With dark doubts sometimes crossing his mind respecting Dora Bouverie's intentions towards him, Mr. St. George nevertheless experienced far more happiness than anxiety during the first few days of that visit to Halesby. It was lovely bracing weather, and the party enjoyed themselves as much as could be expected; of course, there was the usual amount of *ennui* at times, especially among the ladies, who were not out-of-doors as much as the gentlemen; and there were intervals of dulness, especially in the early part of each day, experienced by those who had no intellectual resources.

Ellinor generally read a good deal in the morning after breakfast, or went out to visit the poor people whom Lady Halesby had introduced to her notice. She did not observe that Dora kept very much aloof from her, seldom coming out of her room till late in the day, except for breakfast, and then, perhaps, only appearing when dressed to take a drive out. Her anxiety had not been in any way excited about her sister, and, therefore, she did not perceive anything in her manner or appearance to awaken fears.

In the driving or walking parties that left the house, Mr. St. George generally managed to be the companion of Dora, and sometimes they walked out alone in the still woods, never weary of each other's presence.

" I think I shall never be as happy again as I am now," she said one day, as they were coming towards the house after one of their solitary rambles. " I feel as if some dreadful fate was hanging over me; yet I am determined to enjoy every minute of the present, and to leave the future to itself. I am not given to anticipating miseries."

" Pardon me, but I must say I think you make a mistake there. You are always speaking of evil presentiments and forebodings," said Mr. St. George, smiling.

" Yes, I speak of them, but I do not suffer from them. Before a week passes I shall probably have to go through one of the greatest trials that anyone has ever had to endure, and yet no person, not even my own sister, suspects it."

Mr. St. George looked rather surprised.

" And how long will the trial that you speak
of last ?" he asked.

" It is quite uncertain. It may be the commencement of an eternity of misery, or it may
be ended quite quickly."

" You will let me know how it ter-
minates ?"

" Perhaps I may. You remember I
promised to give you a decisive answer
about that time, and my answer all depends
upon that."

And in this way Dora used to perplex and
mystify her. lover, never, however, for the
purpose of tormenting him, but rather to prepare him for what disappointment might be
coming to him.

One night soon after the arrival of the
guests at Halesby a ball was given there, and
to this ball the neighbouring gentry were
invited. Sir Ralph Barnard and his daughter
likewise were among the company asked from
Norham, and they came to Halesby, neither
being aware that the Miss Bouveries were actually staying in the house till they arrived at the
ball. Both were greatly discomfited at this
revelation; and when the General beheld his
aide-de-camp paying the same attention to

Dora Bouverie as had so annoyed him at the parties at his own house, he determined to write on the spot to Mrs. St. George, and warn her of her son's imminent danger.

Can anybody tell if such interference as this, in love affairs, ever produces a successful result? Sir Ralph had great faith in its efficacy; and the very day after the ball he dispatched a letter to Gartoquil, county Donegal, Ireland, telling the rector's wife that Rodney was engaged in a most alarming flirtation with a girl of no pretensions whatever—a girl without twopence (in his indignation he had brought the dowry down from sixpence), and saying that he was convinced the young man would be mad enough to propose for her, if he were not prevented at once. He then suggested that Mrs. St. George should request her son on some pretext to obtain leave of absence, and join her immediately at Gartoquil, or go to travel with her. Let her say she must spend the remainder of the winter in Italy, and have him for an escort. Let her propose any scheme rather than that such a fine, handsome young fellow should be thrown away on a nobody. Sir Ralph said he would get some one else to do Rodney's duty in

M 5

his absence; and a few months of separation
would surely be enough to put ' a girl like
that' out of Rodney's head.

Upon receiving that terrible epistle, Mrs.
St. George consulted her husband, and consulted the head of the family, Lord Killeevan
—heads of families who have got the estates
being always supposed to possess an extraordinary amount of discernment and sound
sense in matters relating to the affairs of the
other branches; and his lordship said of
course it was a most unpleasant piece of
business, and that it came from young men
in the army being thrown into all sorts of
company in country towns. But he did
not suggest any particular remedy; he merely
assented to everything his sister-in-law
proposed, and she left him, feeling that he
was a man of very shrewd judgment indeed.

In the midst of their happiness, with every
facility for meeting each day as if they were
members of one home, Rodney St. George
and Dora Bouverie were doomed to be
separated. Before the week so much prized
was out, a letter arrived at Halesby from Mrs.
St. George, stating that she wished particu-

larly to see him, that he must come to Gartoquil at once, and that she had written to
General Barnard to get leave for him without
delay. It was a vague letter, explaining
nothing clearly, and for that reason likely to
awaken some uneasiness in Rodney's mind.
It was nearly as unsatisfactory as a telegram,
but it served its purpose. He was a good
son, and no desperation of love could make
him forget the duty he owed to his father and
mother; therefore, he must hasten to Norham and get his servant to pack up with all
speed.

Every one at Halesby was sorry to hear
that he was going away. People liked him
generally. Even the young men, who knew
that he was better looking than themselves,
forgave his personal attractions in consideration of his pleasant manners.

Dora Bouverie was walking out when the
fatal despatch reached her lover, and for some
time he could not find her to tell her of it;
but at last he beheld a glimpse of her through
the leafless trees of a secluded spot where she
often rambled alone. " I have just heard that
I must go to Ireland," he said, when he joined
her; " but I trust I may not be long away.

My mother has written to urge me to set off
for home without any delay."

" I hope there is no illness in your family,"
replied Dora, growing very pale. " I am so
sorry you are going just now, when, perhaps, we may never be under the same roof
again."

" What gloomy views you take of everything ! It all remains in your own power as
to how we shall meet next. You know what
my feelings are, and I shall never change."

" I am afraid people forget in spite of
themselves. Remember, I have not bound
you to anything. I could never bear to be
loved in a half-and-half sort of way, or merely
from any feeling of honour. If you find
yourself repenting of anything you have said
to me, never deceive me ; tell me truthfully
that you wish to give me up, and do not think I
shall ever consider you in any way to blame."

" But why do you speak in this way, when
I assure you that my regard for you must be
unalterable ?" asked the young man, in a
slightly offended tone. " I have never loved
anyone but you ; I am not of a fickle nature.
I do not deserve such an opinion as you seem
to entertain of me."

"I believe that you care a great deal for me now," said Dora; "but I also believe that there is a great deal of truth in the old saying, 'Out of sight, out of mind.' People cannot control their own hearts—they are not responsible for the changes that sometimes take place in their feelings; and, at all events, you cannot hold yourself in any way bound to me till I give you a decisive answer as to what I shall be able to do myself."

"Then you will write to me, if I am detained longer in Ireland than I expect to be?"

"Yes; give me your address, and I will promise to let you hear from me."

"And I am to be permitted to write to you in the first instance?"

"I should like you to do so, but it would be better for you not to write to me—much better; I shall not ask it."

The more averse Dora was to holding her lover to any binding promises of attachment, the more he felt inclined to regard her as a prize that might never, perhaps, be his.

"If anything should occur to prevent my writing to you, what should you think?" she added, after a pause.

" I should fear the worst; that you never cared for me."

" But you know anything might happen to keep me from writing as soon as I could wish. However, in case I do write, you will surely answer me quickly—that is, if my letter requires a reply ?"

" I shall send you an answer immediately," he said, as he took out his card-case, and wrote his address in pencil on the back of a card.

" In some respects I am a very exacting person," she said, as she took the card and read the direction given to her; " and if I did not hear from you the very day I expected, I should feel intensely miserable—intensely unforgiving, too."

" And yet you expect me to forgive you everything; you even throw out hints of never writing to me at all."

" But I am a woman. It is much harder for a woman to overlook slights and negligences from a man than it is for him to bear such things from her. If I write first to you I shall be making a great concession—doing something that is not usual for a lady to do in such a case ; and for that reason I shall

expect a great deal in return—I mean a great
deal of courtesy and consideration."

" But you will not let me write first to you ?"

" No, certainly not. I shall send you a
letter unless something unforseen occurs, and
if I ask you for a speedy answer, remember
that I will not pardon you if you do not send
it."

He assured her that she need not fear any
negligence on his part, and repeated former
declarations of fervent attachment, thinking
at the same time that she was rather unreasonable, and difficult to comprehend.

She permitted him to press her hand to his
lips, and they parted without any more conversation. He was obliged to hurry at once
to Norham ; she remained out of doors
till the agitation of the leave-taking was over.

" Is my last glimpse of happiness departed
now ?" she asked herself when he was gone.
" Does anything seem to tell me that I shall
ever see him again with the same feelings as
now ?"

The wind sighed in the treetops, and the
bare branches stirred with a faint rustle, but
there was no whisper of comfort for the ears
or the heart of Dora Bouverie.

CHAPTER XV.

A NEW ARRIVAL AT HALESBY.

THE very same day that Mr. St. George left
Halesby the party there received the addition
of another person, whose arrival caused a
great deal of surprise to several people. Just
about dinner hour, in the darkness of the
winter evening a fly drove up the avenue,
and stopped before the house, and out of it
came an aristocratic-looking young man, with
his arm in a sling, and a great deal of
muffling round his neck. Paying the fly-man
liberally, and dismissing him a little haughtily,
he mounted the hall-door steps, and rang for
admission.

The footman opening the door stared a
little at him, but, quickly recognizing him,
smiled, and bade him welcome, ushering him
in with an air of alacrity. Other servants,
meeting him, smiled graciously also, and said

Mr. Lyon would be glad to see him; and finally everybody, high and low, in the house, knew that Mr. Dawson Bouverie had unexpectedly made his appearance at Halesby.

Hearing that her brother had come, Ellinor ran out to meet him before he was fit to be seen in the drawing-room, and of course expressed great satisfaction that he had arrived.

"Oh, I thought I might as well come on here as stay at home in that stupid hole, Evergreen," he answered, without returning any of her expressions of pleasure at meeting him—" our father seems to have grown so intolerably disagreeable, and my mother more moping than ever."

"When did you get to Norham?" asked Ellinor, a little sadly.

" Yesterday, and I have not been very well of late—hurt my arm, and got the back of my head bruised by an accident, and altogether feel rather seedy. What sort of people are here?   Is the place as humdrum as ever ?"

" There is a charming party staying with us.   I hope you will like the people."

" I don't know, I'm sure," replied Dawson,

in a tone as if he did not much care either.
"I am scarcely fit for company, have had a
bad sore throat—obliged to muffle, you see,
and I should much prefer being without these
people staying in the house. Will they go
away soon?"

"Oh, not for some days. I thought you
said the place was humdrum in its usual quiet
state."

"I am sure I don't know what I said, but
I know what I think. I suppose I may ring
for some brandy and water."

Ellinor said she supposed he could, and felt
concerned that he should feel in need of any
stimulant when he had only driven from
Norham. She feared he had been weakened
by some serious illness or accident which he
had not mentioned to his family. He seemed
out of temper, and ruder even than he usually
was to his sisters, though he never was very
polite to them. His best manner towards
them was generally one of indifference.
Neither of them could remember a time when
he had obliged them in any way, or paid
them even the attention of listening with any
interest to what they said to him, unless it
happened to be something concerning himself.

When Dawson said he supposed he could ring for brandy and water, Ellinor thought she should leave him to make his arrangements for dinner, and as soon as she was gone, the first thing he did was to take from his neck the woollen comforter which had been wound round it, and to lay bare his throat, and look at it in the glass by the light of the wax candles burning brightly round it. The marks of five distinct bruises, such as might have been given by five powerful fingers pressed violently on the flesh—the flesh not being broken, but of a red and blue colour — appeared on the throat thus exposed to view, and there was some degree of swelling, and a good deal of pain in the surrounding parts. To hide these ugly marks on his throat was the young man's chief care, and, by a dexterous arrangement of a more than usually voluminous necktie, he was enabled to present a tolerable appearance, such as might not attract particular notice. With the rest of his toilet he was likewise painstaking; and though one arm seemed a good deal disabled he preferred dressing himself to accepting the proffered assistance of the servant who had been deputed to see to his wants.

On making his appearance in the drawing-
room his aspect was that of a very fashionable,
elegant young man, with manners perfectly
well bred. There was no gruffness now, no
ill-tempered tone of voice, no indifference to
what anybody said. Dawson's company-air
was rather a gentle, indolent one ; and his
dark hazel eyes glanced softly around with a
winning expression that beguiled many people
into believing him to be the most amiable of
mortals. If a Lavater had been among the
company assembled in the room he might
probably have discovered some lines about
his face indicative of defects in the disposition
and character, but common-place mortals saw
nothing in young Bouverie's face that was not
agreeable and handsome. Lady Halesby
welcomed him cordially, and the viscount
himself was equally glad to see him. Gerard
Lyon had already greeted him before he appeared in the drawing-room with much
warmth and heartiness; and they had talked
a little business matter over in a way very
satisfactory to Dawson—that is, if he was in a
state of mind to be satisfied with anything.

Dora Bouverie received her brother coolly
enough—quite as coolly as he met her. She

was nearly as selfish as he was, but not quite; and she could not forget that he was concerned in the unpleasant dilemma in which she was placed at present respecting Mr. Clarke. She was not one of the estimable women in the world who believe that the male members of families require, and are entitled to, a great amount of soothing, and comforting, and petting from their female relatives, on account of some imaginary hardships in their lot. It was Dora's conviction that her brother had got decidedly more of the world's luck, so far, than she or Ellinor had, and that he was very well able to solace himself, without any help from her. He had never been obliged to do his own tailoring, or his own mending of dilapidated garments, and he had possessed a good deal of independent money since he was a mere boy; he would not be obliged to marry somebody or anybody for a provision, whether he liked to marry or not; and if he had to live in camp at Aldershott, with its *désagrémens* of dulness, drill, and mice running over him in bed, as he described it, he was paid for it. His endurances were not like those of women, who have to bear unknown troubles without getting any pecuniary

reward, or much soothing or petting either.
Besides, he was not always at Aldershott, or
with his regiment at any military station. He
was often on leave, nobody knew exactly
where; sometimes in the Highlands of Scot-
land, sometimes on the Continent. He had
once set up a small yacht, and gone up the
Mediterranean with friends, and his family
knew nothing of the trip till he wrote to them
from Corsica. Altogether Dora considered
that she was not by any means called upon
to minister comfort to her brother; and so
she said, " How do you do?" to him somewhat indifferently, and never asked him
how he had come, or how long he should
stay, or appeared at all more interested in
him than if she was the brother, and he the
sister; and yet I am bound to say that Dawson liked her just as well as he liked Ellinor.

Lady Mary Shelbank, the pink-com-
plexioned, somewhat plain young girl, who
was staying with her grand-parents at Halesby,
happened to be an heiress and an orphan,
and when young Mr. Bouverie found this out
he put on his most fascinating expression of
dark hazel eye, and made himself extremely
agreeable. He had all the air of a man who

had plenty of money, because he never denied himself anything that money or credit could give him. Since he went to Eton his acquaintances had chiefly been among the highest classes of society; and though he was neither good-hearted nor clever, he had many friends still among those who had been his school companions. It was his aim to imitate the dress and expenditure of men who had thousands a year, and in this way he ran into great debt. If Lady Mary Shelbank had not been so "confoundedly ugly," he thought, there might be something really amusing in getting up a flirtation with her. Strictly speaking, Dawson Bouverie was not what is called a lady's man; he criticised women very severely—which a genuine lady's man never does. He required a girl to be very handsome indeed before he would deign to admire her; she must dress well, too, and be of good family—"up to the mark," as he expressed it, in every way. All that Lady Mary wanted was the beauty; but, then, she had the high birth and a large fortune coming to her in a year or two. She might be a good "spec.," plain as she was; so he took her down to dinner with great alacrity when Lady Halesby

told him, and he talked sweetly to her, and
looked into her green-grey eyes, as if he had
never seen such heavenly orbs before. Ellinor
was pleased to see that he made himself
agreeable at Halesby; she would have been
greatly grieved if he had offended or displeased her kind friends in any way. She
was living at this time herself in an atmosphere of happiness. Every day she was
recovering from the depression of spirits
which the late troubles in her own home had
caused her, and she felt very thankful.

"Do I deserve the peace of mind I enjoy
now?" she sometimes asked herself; "and
shall I have to go back again to the misery I
have for a time escaped from?"

Whatever might come for her, she felt that
she must be resigned and brave. Her heart
was at Halesby, and she knew it would remain there when she left the place. Glimpses
of a prosperous and a happy future were
opened to her view day after day; but still
there was nothing certain in them, and she
shrank from deciding anything, even in her
own mind.

After Dawson Bouverie's arrival at Halesby
the weather grew rainy and stormy, and there

were no out-of-door excursions for the ladies. As to the young man himself, he did not feel disposed for any great amount of exertion ; he got up late in the morning, played billiards, looked over the newspapers, and was ill at ease. He scarcely liked being at Halesby, but he disliked Evergreen still more. His father's conversation was not agreeable to him, and his mother's silence and frequent sighs were most unpleasant.

People were beginning to get a little tired of this visit to Halesby, and some were thinking of going away. Mrs. Carpendale felt somewhat discontented, because her number and variety of dresses were much behind those of Mrs. Vansen Hopwood: she had sang all her best songs and played all her best pieces over and over again, till she felt that those who heard them so often must be well nigh sick of them; and therefore she was growing *ennuyée* and bored, and she told her husband it was time for them to go back to Norham ; and he, having been dreadfully bored after the first day or two, gladly assented that it was; so that the party was lessened of this happy couple. Next day some more people took their departure, in-

cluding the two young officers quartered at
Norham; and there seemed a general disposition among the guests to break up and go
home. The dull, wet weather appeared to
chill everybody. Lady Halesby felt rheumatic twinges flying through her frame; her
husband feared for the wellbeing of his wheat
and oats that had just been sown upon a new
plan which the rain might defeat. There
could be no hunting for the gentlemen, no
drives for the ladies. People looked in vain
at the barometer for any hope ; for though the
glass sometimes was reported to be "going
up," the rain continued to come down without, in the least, attending to such prognosti-
cations. Dora Bouverie's solitary walks in
the leafless groves were at an end; she felt
most wretched, and filled with conflicting
emotions. Listening to the rain dripping
ceaselessly from the branches of trees, and
the wind wailing mournfully round the great
towers of the house, she seemed to hear the
voice of doom through all the dreary sounds,
yet she was making up her mind to work out
a fate for herself—to fight desperately against
all her dark forebodings of an evil destiny.
She would not sit still, and allow herself to

be plunged in misery for the rest of her life; she would resist to the utmost, and give up home and family, if need be, to accomplish her own ends.

The thoughts of going home and meeting Mr. Clarke grew hourly more intolerable to her. She could not persuade herself any longer that her regard for Mr. St. George was a trifling one. Those past few days of seeing each other so constantly had strengthened all the feelings that she had before entertained for him. The time had come for her to love most earnestly and disinterestedly, without a thought of worldliness, and she determined to abandon all idea of being raised up by marriage to any remarkably high position, though she knew well that if she had only wished it she might have married highly before the present time, and could, no doubt, have opportunities of doing so again ; the winning of a suitor was a very easy matter with her—so easy, that in general she scarcely valued the prize. But now she was won herself, and she would sacrifice much for her lover. She would make up her mind to be poor as his wife, and to reform from her thoughtless, selfish ways of old.

She would try to make herself as good as he
thought she was, that he might not be disappointed in after days.

"If I marry him I may grow better and
wiser," she thought; "but if I marry anyone
else I shall grow worse than I am even now,
and I am too portionless and poor to be able
to live without marrying at all."

So reasoning in this way she came to the
conclusion that her prospects of ever becoming
a happy or a good woman were concerned in
her present determination. She would refuse
Mr. Clarke's proposal, decidedly and irrevo-
cably. No persuasion of father or mother,
brother or sister, would induce her to alter
that resolution; and she would write there at
Halesby to Mr. St. George, before she would
run the risk of seeing again either her father
or the barrack-master, and tell him distinctly
what she meant to do. All wavering would
be at an end then. She should, at least, be
able to let her lover know that she fully returned his regard for her.

As she had herself foreseen, it was not an
easy matter for her to write that letter to Mr.
St. George, and she regretted that she had
not permitted him to write first to her. Yet,

still, she had promised to let him know her answer in writing, and, in spite of her scruples, she must do it. How much she would have given for Ellinor's help in the composition of that remarkable letter; but she was not to be confided in till the matter should be settled, and then Ellinor might give her up, or still treat her with affection, just as she liked.

In the composition and execution of her intended letter to Mr. St. George, Dora made many delays and many copies. She wished to write in such a way as would convey the full extent of her regard for him, and at the same time be in her own estimation perfectly dignified; and she found this a somewhat difficult task, so that the time was going by, and still the important missive was not dispatched.

One afternoon of the rainy time we have mentioned, she was busily occupied in her perplexing task, when, to her surprise, Ellinor entered her room where she was writing. She started as her sister came in, and in some confusion threw a sheet of blotting paper over her letter, not perceiving at first that

Ellinor's face wore a look of the most intense
consternation, and that her eyes seemed
nearly twice their usual size.

For some time her sister did not utter any
word ; she seemed bewildered, and as if
stricken by some great misfortune.

" Are you ill, Ellinor ?" asked Dora, in
some alarm, as she arose from the table at
which she was sitting.

" No, not very; I have come to say that
we must leave Halesby to-night.   I must go
home immediately."

" Home ! Oh, something wretched has happened !   Have you heard from mamma or
papa ?"

" No; there is nothing wrong at home, but
we are to go from this to-night, and we must
pack up at once."

Ellinor spoke decidedly, and not in her
usual tone of voice.   Dora thought it seemed
a harsh, strange tone, and she was surprised.
Her conscience, too, felt a little uneasy.
Could her sister's peculiar manner be caused
by any discovery she had made concerning
the business that was occupying her own
mind so exclusively ?   But would that ac-

count for the extreme pallor of Ellinor's face, the dark shadows under her eyes, the wild, startled look of her countenance, and the limp, powerless way her hands seemed to hang by her sides?

In the next chapter I must begin to say something of what had occurred a few hours earlier during that remarkable day at Halesby.

CHAPTER XVI.

LADY HALESBY READS THE LETTERS OF RACHEL
HAMMERSLY'S BETRAYER.

In the midst of more enticing duties, Ellinor
Bouverie had never forgotten the young
woman, whom we have hitherto known as
Rebecca Hammond, during the stay of the
gay visitors at Halesby. She visited her
nearly every day; and the girl had, at length,
expressed her wish to relieve her kind bene-
factors of the burden she felt herself to be
upon them. Miss Bouverie's conversation
and advice had been of great use to her in
calming down many of her dangerous, wild
thoughts, and in giving her some degree of
hope that she might yet retrieve her character,
and make amends for her past misconduct.
She had already confided to both Lady
Halesby and Ellinor that her real name was
Rachel Hammersly, not Rebecca Hammond,

and that her uncle's farm, the Priory, lay in
Shropshire. This revelation, of course, the
reader made for himself or herself long since;
but though it seemed an important one to the
poor girl herself, it failed to make any particular difference to Lady Halesby or Miss
Bouverie.

Lady Halesby sometimes of late was un-
accompanied by Ellinor when she walked
down to the gate-lodge; and one day when
she was thus alone Rachel, after some hesitation, placed in her hands for the first time the
letters that her dishonourable lover had
written to her, as likewise the picture of himself which he had given to her.

" I have told you my name, my lady, and
I must not conceal anything further from
you," she said. "These are the letters I
received from that base young man, and also
the little scrap of paper which I picked up,
and which turned out to be part of a letter
written to him mentioning that he would be
expected at a certain time at Norham, which
was the reason I took the trouble of coming
into this neighbourhood."

" Very well," said Lady Halesby. "I
shall read them over, as you wish it, when I

N 5

have leisure." So she took the little parcel of letters and the picture and went back to the house. For some time after that her attention was called away to the entertainment of her guests, and she laid the letters aside in a drawer, intending to read them some other day. When that other day arrived, which happened in the rainy weather that occurred after Dawson Bouverie's arrival at Halesby, and while he was trying to amuse himself by flirting with Lady Mary Shelbank, and other guests were going away, Lady Halesby was very much surprised, indeed, and felt somewhat as if her senses were forsaking her. She read the letters, examined the handwritings of them and of the scrap of torn letter which had been instrumental in bringing Rachel Hammersly to the neighbourhood of Norham, and then took the portrait of Mr. Dormer—Rachel's miserable betrayer—out of its case, and stared at it, till her dim, cold eyes seemed to light up with a fire that rarely shone in them, and her lips became compressed with a strange rigidity.

" This cannot be," she murmured, laying her hand on her forehead ; " I must surely be under some delusion."

And the longer she gazed at the letters and the picture the more confused she grew, till at last she felt the necessity of setting them all aside, and trying to think of something else. A rheumatic headache kept her confined to her own rooms for the rest of that day ; but before the next morning she determined to try an experiment that would put an end to her doubts at once.

Ellinor Bouverie had rarely felt happier than she did at this time ; she was full of hope and peace of mind. Her health had physically improved since her arrival at Halesby, and the wretched feeling of depression and nervousness which had so often oppressed her at home seemed to have departed almost entirely.

In the early part of that day to which I alluded at the end of the last chapter, she and Gerard Lyon were alone in the library at Halesby. She had been reading, as was her custom, for an hour or two before luncheon, and he had joined her. At first he spoke of a few indifferent matters, and then he became silent, with a restless, undecided air as if he wished to give utterance to some particular thoughts, yet scarcely knew how to commence.

"We have had a delightful visit," said
Ellinor. "I shall be quite sorry when Dora
and I are to go home. I am afraid I have
been spoiled here."

And she laughed.

"Or rather you have spoiled others," returned Gerard, earnestly. "You have been
yourself, like a ray of sunshine, all the time
bringing light everywhere. I shall be very
sad, indeed, when you leave us, unless I can
hope for a time when you will soon return.
You know, Ellinor, I am sure, how much you
are to me, and I have sometimes flattered myself that you were not indifferent——"

The entrance of a servant interrupted the
continuance of this speech, which, if it had
been then finished, might have made such a
difference to Ellinor.   He came to say Lady
Halesby wished to see Miss Bouverie ; and
then he began to put coals on the fire, and
sweep up the cinders from the hearth, and
bustled about so long that there was no hope
of getting rid of him in any reasonable length
of time.

Nevertheless, Ellinor was flushed and
happy, proud and joyous, and very thankful.
Worldly prosperity of the highest kind seemed

to be awaiting her, and, above all, the person
whose good opinion she so warmly prized—
whose love she felt she could return with the
deepest feeling of sincerity—had at last
spoken to her almost decidedly ; she felt certain that only for the interruption occasioned
by the servant he would have made an un-
mistakeable declaration of attachment to her.
And in that conviction she was right.   But
the servant had made the interruption, and
smaller events than that have decided the fate
of people far greater than she was.

She got up to leave the room and join Lady
Halesby, her step being so light and her heart
so glad, that she seemed to tread on air.   She
found her hostess sitting, with her bonnet and
shawl on, in the ante-room of one of the
drawing-rooms.

"I hope your headache is better," said
Ellinor, tenderly, as she approached her.

"Not much," replied Lady Halesby,
coldly.   "I want you to come with me to
the lodge gate.   Have you ever seen the
letters Rachel Hammersly's lover wrote to
her ?"

"No," said Ellinor; "I never liked to ask
for them."

"And you never saw her lover's picture?"

"No; she never offered to let me see it."

"Well, I have the letters and the picture here," said Lady Halesby, holding up the little parcel; "and by-and-bye you shall see them."

Ellinor could not help remarking that her hostess seemed less courteous and kind in her manner to her than usual, and just now she felt a little sensitive on the subject. If she were to look coldly upon her, what hope could she entertain of being received with a warm welcome at Halesby at any future time?

Ellinor had not been for more than a fortnight there without discovering how great was the influence that the mother had over her only son—her only child, upon whom all her maternal affection had been lavished since his birth.

There were times when Miss Bouverie felt doubtful of her hostess possessing really tender feelings for the generality of individuals. Charitable, and apparently kind, she certainly was; but there seemed a want somewhere. In act Lady Halesby was always benevolent, yet Ellinor felt sometimes disappointed that

there was not more softness of look and
speech—something less hard and sternly
dutiful in what was done or said by her kinswoman.

They both walked down to the gate lodge
slowly. The morning was damp, but not
rainy just then. Lady Halesby looked at her
watch pretty often, and then generally
slackened her pace. She scarcely spoke at
all. Was she a capricious woman, prone to
unaccountable fits of ill-humour?

Arriving at the gate lodge, Lady Halesby
desired Ellinor to stay back for a minute or
two, while she should go in and speak alone
with Rachel. Mrs. M'Stare was not at home
at this time ; the lodge was in sole possession
of the young woman, who listened to what
her protectress said to her in much agitation,
and with some incredulity; but Lady Halesby
considered that it was better to prepare
her mind for what was coming than run the
risk of startling her too abruptly in her present weak state of health. After speaking
with her for about seven or eight minutes she
returned to Ellinor and said she might now
enter the lodge, and again took out her watch
and looked at it. Happy and buoyant as

Ellinor had been half an hour before, she felt quite damped in spirit now, and she could only address a few commonplace observations to Rachel, who appeared more than usually excited and nervous. Lady Halesby maintained a strict silence as she kept looking out of the lattice window of the lodge parlour, with rapt attention. Ellinor had her back to the window, and did not know how fixedly her hostess was staring out, evidently watching for something, or some one. It was altogether a time of constraint, by no means agreeable to Miss Bouverie, who hoped it might soon terminate ; but Lady Halesby showed no disposition to leave the lodge quickly; she kept her place at the window steadily, while Rachel continued her needlework with trembling finger, and very bewildered thoughts. At length there were footsteps heard approaching—the sound of a man's tread grating on the gravelled walk outside. Lady Halesby gave one of her stern coughs, and now quitting her position at the window, left the lodge, while Rachel laid down her work, and looked fixedly at Miss Bouverie, without uttering a word.

Ellinor wondered if she should also leave

the gate lodge, and was thinking of going away, when Lady Halesby returned, accompanied by the person whose footsteps had been heard a few minutes before, and for whom she had evidently been watching. To her surprise Miss Bouverie beheld in this person her own brother.

"Now, Rachel Hammersly," said Lady Halesby, in a harsh, stern voice, "you can say if you ever saw this gentleman before."

The girl neither shrieked nor fainted, nor uttered a stifled cry or moan; but she stood up and stared at Dawson Bouverie for nearly two minutes, without uttering a word.

"Speak out," said Lady Halesby; "you can surely say yes or no."

Ellinor was astonished, and looked from one to the other of the three people before her.

Her brother looked pale; his face wore a supercilious expression, and a slight smile curled his lip.

"Yes, my lady, I have seen him," said Rachel, at last, "he is the person whom I was acquainted with as Mr. Dormer, at Pentley and in London." And then she flashed a defiant wild look from her black eyes at the young man, which might have burned into his soul, had he not been proof even against their fire.

"I don't understand this, really," said Dawson, without faltering in his tone. "What does the young woman mean?"

"She means," replied Lady Halesby, "that you are the person who made false promises to her—who seduced her into trusting your word, and then led her to commit a most dishonourable and iniquitous crime!"

"Upon my honour, this is most amusing!" he said, looking round with an air of surprise. "The girl is evidently deranged. What is the name she called me by a minute ago?"

"The name you called yourself by not long since," returned Lady Halesby, drawing a little packet from her pocket; "the name you have signed to your letters to her, which I hold in my hand."

"And you are so credulous, Lady Halesby, as to believe this?" asked Dawson.

"I believe it fully. Even if I did not know your own handwriting, I could not be mistaken in the writing of your sister, who is here beside you. Come, Miss Bouverie, and

look at these letters," continued Lady
Halesby, who was trembling with indignation—"I do not suppose that *you* will deny
the truth !"

Amazed and bewildered, Ellinor now went
forward and took the letters in her hand.
Her eyes wandered over the writing—the
words seemed to dance and flicker in her
gaze.

"You cannot deny that these letters are in
your brother's handwriting—that this picture
in my hand is his picture, or that this scrap
of writing is your own," continued Lady
Halesby. " The picture I particularly know,
because it was taken at Halesby at the same
time that my son's miniature was taken by
the same artist."

" What an absurd row about nothing !"
exclaimed young Bouverie impatiently, as he
now comprehended that he could not presume
to screen himself any longer by falsehood.
"Even if I did write these letters, and call
myself by any name I pleased, I do not see
that anyone has a right to question me upon
the subject. This young woman has herself
to blame for entering into a correspondence
that may have raised false hopes. If she

chose to write to me, I suppose it was to be expected that I should answer her."

" You know my story, Lady Halesby," said Rachel, proudly ; " and I need not refute anything that this man says. If you believe what I have already told you, there can be no necessity for me to repeat anything of it here, and if you do *not* believe it, then there will be no use in my trying to be credited in anything I may say now."

" I believe your word," replied Lady Halesby. " I do not doubt anything you have said—though God knows I have got reason enough to doubt the truth and honesty of every one ! Miss Bouverie, is not that part of a letter you wrote to your brother expressing a wish to see him during the last Christmas at Norham ?"

Ellinor raised her agitated face, and answered in the affirmative. She could not persuade herself that it was any other than her own hand which had written those few lines—" If you come to Norham about Christmas, as we hope you will, I should like you to stay a long time."

And those few words written so unconsciously, had been the means of tracking her brother out, and bringing him into well-merited disgrace and condemnation—they were the means of filling her own heart with shame and misery. Heaven alone could tell with what misery!

"And is he *her* brother?" asked Rachel, lifting up her hands as she saw the expression of the wretched sister's face. "Is she, who has been like an angel of mercy to me, so nearly related to such a being?"

"I suppose I may go now?" said Dawson haughtily, as he prepared to put on his hat.

"Not quite so fast, if you please," returned Lady Halesby. "You must first explain if you intend to make any reparation to this young woman for the guilt you have plunged her into—if you mean to pay the money back that she procured for you by forgery and falsehood?"

"I do not comprehend what you mean. If she has been guilty of forgery and falsehood, that is not my affair."

"You deny your share in that crime also?"

"This whole business appears a most contemptible farce!" exclaimed the young man, insolently. "I wonder any one of your sense could put faith in what a person of that girl's character says, Lady Halesby. Who would credit her oath? But ladies do not understand these matters; they are full of enthusiasm often about the most worthless of their sex. Ellinor, I should say you would be all the better if out of this atmosphere. I had no idea you had found such a creature to waste your charity upon!"

"You and your sister may go as soon as you please," said Lady Halesby, sternly. "I shall not seek to detain you any longer. Rachel Hammersly, you need not mention this meeting to any one about the place. You see you can expect nothing from your betrayer; he does not even display any feeling of shame or remorse. For the sake of his unfortunate mother, who is related to Lord Halesby, I do not wish the matter to be publicly spoken of; but you may still rely on my countenance and support. Miss Bouverie, can you let me have a few words with you?"

Miss Bouverie—Ellinor no longer!

Dawson, trying to smile pityingly at the whole proceeding, yet looking rather pale, walked away with an air of indifference; and

his sister stayed behind to hear what Lady
Halesby wished to say to her.

They walked slowly back to the house, and
Lady Halesby spoke thus as they went
on :—

" I cannot think it possible, Miss Bouverie,
that you were unaware of the principles of
your brother, after so many years of intercourse with him ; and yet you told me here,
not long ago, that he had very high feelings of honour.   Now, is it credible that you
could have been deceived so far in his
character?"

" I assure you I was quite unaware of
what he has proved himself capable of,"
replied Ellinor, trying to speak as firmly as
she could. " I truly believed whatever I said
to you of him."

" That may or may not be the case," returned Lady Halesby, in the dry, hard tone
that her young relative had often heard her
speak in to others, but never before to herself ; " but you can hardly get me to credit
that he ever was an amiable or well-disposed
boy or youth in your domestic circle.   This
revelation we have just made of his infamous
conduct (you know yourself that no one could

have thought his treatment of that poor girl, Rachel Hammersly, worse than you did your-self), has made me alter my opinion respecting your whole family. What can I believe of any of you now? How have you all been trained up? What have your parents been about? A whisper of any misconduct, any display of ill-principle on the part of your brother, never reached me. Whatever you must have known him in your heart to be you kept it a secret. I feel that there was no real confidence in me; I feel that I knew nothing about you—nothing truly but what I know now of your brother!"

Ellinor felt mortified in the extreme; there seemed something almost insolent in her companion's way of speaking, and her pride was hurt—every feeling of her heart was wounded by such words addressed to her.

" I have never deceived you, Lady Halesby," she said. " I never told you what was false. If I did not think my brother a paragon of amiability myself, I surely was not bound to state my opinion of him to any one else. If I had entertained the smallest idea that he was mean or dishonourable, I should never have told you that he had high principles. What earthly motive could I have had in deceiving you about him, or any other member of my family ?"

" If you had motive in it, of course you understand what that motive was," returned Lady Halesby. " This much I can assure you of, that you would never have been invited on terms of intimacy to my house had I not believed you to be a most truthful, straightforward person, a high-minded, high-principled gentlewoman, incapable of doing or saying what was false. I have watched you narrowly—purposely watched you to test your disposition—for the last fortnight and upwards, and I thought I read your character clearly; but I confess I feel staggered now : I have lost all faith in my own judgment. Therefore I will not press you or your sister to continue your visit to Halesby. As to your wretched brother, of course he will leave this instantly."

Ellinor knew that her hostess had often been guilty of addressing to others what had seemed to her very harsh, rude speeches, but she had never yet spoken to herself in any way that was uncourteous till the present moment. Hard thoughts of her came into her head—angry thoughts even ; for Ellinor was merely human, and her spirit had been sorely tried. She was offended deeply.

" I shall certainly leave Halesby instantly, also," she said, as the colour flushed up over her pallid face. "Dora and I shall return home this evening."

"Just as you like," said the implacable woman beside her, without betraying a shade of softened feeling.

Then they walked on in silence which remained unbroken even till they reached the house, parting in the hall. Ellinor went to her own room, feeling as if in a dreadful dream. The darkest shadow that had ever in her life clouded her spirit was over it now. When the first burst of her indignation against Lady Halesby had subsided, she fell into a state of the utmost despair. Her brother to have turned out such a reprobate ! To have disgraced his whole family—to have injured herself irreparably ! It was, indeed, true that she herself had pointed out the baseness of the supposed Dormer to Lady Halesby in the most vivid manner. Only for herself Dawson's shameful dishonour might have never been

known in that neighbourhood. A letter of
her own had been the means of bringing
Rachel Hammersly towards Norham; her
own handwriting had been as an avenger, and
as a bringing of the culprit to judgment! In
the agony of her reflections Ellinor was
scarcely reasonable; she blamed herself as
being the cause of this terrible discovery of
her brother's iniquity; she was nearly wild
with shame and horror. And then, how
cruel it seemed of Lady Halesby to bring her,
in such a cold-blooded manner, to the gate
lodge, and allow her to become aware of
Dawson's ill conduct, without the slightest
preparation. Were those people right who
thought that woman had no truly kind feeling—no real charity; that she was merely
trying to work out some poor false scheme of
mistaken piety by dead works—the building
of churches—the giving away of alms?
Would any person of common good-nature
have exposed a sister to such a trial as she
had made her undergo that day, and then addressed to her such rude, such mortifying,
sentences? Should she ever be able to think
of the mistress of Halesby in future with any
feelings but those of indignation and anger?

Would her stony eyes haunt her for ever, as the eyes of some soulless spectre?

Ellinor's thoughts were very hard; for she was sorely stricken. She felt that the one happy dream of her life had passed away for ever—the only ray of light that had come through the latter years of her existence had vanished suddenly, and the world must henceforth be dark to her—darker than ever it had seemed before, because the light now extinguished had only made the darkness more intolerable and oppressive.

For two whole hours she remained in her own room, engaged in a most bitter mental strife—such a strife as she never could have supposed herself capable of. All ideas of resignation and submission seemed impossible to her. In the great agony of her soul, she thought that God had forsaken her; and she could utter no prayer.

This state of mind had scarcely subsided when she felt it necessary to go to Dora, and inform her that they must leave Halesby that evening. No wonder she looked wild and terror-stricken—no wonder her sister was startled at her appearance, and at the harsh, strangely-altered tone of her voice.

CHAPTER XVII.

ELLINOR AND DORA BOUVERIE LEAVE
HALESBY.

ELLINOR did not like to inform Dora all at
once of the discovery that had been made
concerning their brother's dishonourable conduct, but she admitted that Lady Halesby had
behaved uncourteously to her, and that it was
impossible for them to remain another night
under her roof; and Dora, having a great
respect for her sister's judgment, instantly
felt that she could not attempt to argue
against her decision, though she by no means
wished to return home so soon. What she
saw of Ellinor's extreme agitation and evident
distress of mind convinced her that she had
very good reason for thus suddenly quitting
Halesby, and Dora was not particularly
curious to ascertain the particulars of what
had annoyed her sister, and led to her resolu-

tion of leaving the house. In general, Dora
Bouverie was not at all inquisitive concerning
the affairs of others, and when she observed that
Ellinor did not herself offer any very minute
explanation of what Lady Halesby had said
or done to offend her, she had tact enough to
abstain from questioning her closely. She
could not help sighing, however, as she prepared to shut up her writing-desk, knowing
that the completion of her important letter to
Mr. St. George must now be deferred for a
day or two, and that she should have to encounter her father before it could finally be
dispatched.

"I shall pack up and prepare to return
home at once, Ellinor," said Dora, who felt
indignant against Lady Halesby, without
knowing the extent of her offence towards her
sister; and Ellinor merely was able to say,

" Very well ; let us be ready to leave at
six o'clock, and I shall send for a fly to the
Halesby Arms, in the town."

" Will you not ask for a carriage from
this—"

" No; certainly not," said Ellinor, de-
cisively. She was in a miserable state of
mind—miserable, because she felt how weak

she was; how unequal to bearing this great
trial with any degree of fortitude. Every
mo ment she was growing more and more
con vi nced of her own want of resignation and
subi ission. And she had presumed often to
lecture and exhort the poor ignorant people
whom she was in the habit of visiting, to bear
their griefs and privations and calamities
with patience, and faith in the wisdom of
Providence, which had appointed them to
suffer and be chastened! She felt humiliated,
and as if she had been a hypocrite—preaching
what she never knew how to practise herself
—what she had never learned to practise. Had
this great stroke come to reveal to her the utter
frailty of her own nature—the uncertain,
tottering foundation of her own faith? Perhaps it had; she may have been too presumptuous, too confident of her own powers
to endure. She was now bewildered, tossed
about on a w ild sea, with no spar of hope to
cling to; a very wretched, weak mortal,
indeed. Without consulting with Lady
Halesby any further, Miss Bouverie sent a
messenger to the town of Halesby, to order a
fly to be in readiness to convey her and Dora
to Evergreen at about six o'clock that even-

ing. She did not wish to encounter another dinner at Halesby. She could not have endured the ordeal of sitting at table with the members of Lord Halesby's family, after what had happened. Above all, she could not have borne to meet Gerard Lyon. Once or twice the idea struck her that she might yet preserve Lady Halesby's favour by writing her a conciliatory letter, explaining how little she ever imagined her brother to be capable of dishonourable behaviour—how completely mistaken she was in his character; but her pride revolted always at the thought of addressing that cruel woman. Even for the sake of her son—even for the sake of those prospects of happiness, and wealth and influence, and power to be of use in the world, which had so lately been before her eyes, but which were all vanishing from her vision now, she could not bring herself to write one sentence of humility or regret. If Dawson had erred, why should Lady Halesby visit misconduct on the rest of his family? If he had acted a dishonourable part, was that any reason for supposing his sisters to be unworthy also? No, Ellinor would not write any conciliatory letter to Lady Halesby; she

would depart from her house, and never more
stand within its walls; she would root up all
remembrances of the past; she would steel
her heart against any lingering affections
connected with the old mansion that had been
so dear to her since childhood. Her life must
begin anew; another existence would open
before her; dark, cheerless, unlit by a ray of
hope, she would give herself up to working
out what she might consider to be her duty
to God and her fellow-creatures; but she
could look for no earthly happiness any more.
If she had never paid that last visit to Halesby,
how much better it would have been!

The packing up of the sisters took only a
short time to accomplish; they did not meet
again till they were nearly ready to leave the
house.

" Is Dawson coming back with us?" asked
Dora, when she and Ellinor had finished their
packing.

" No; I daresay he has already gone. I
am afraid that our brother has been acting
very badly of late. I am afraid he will break
papa's heart."

" What has he been doing?" asked Dora,
rousing herself up more than she might have

done had she not felt how much concerned she was herself in Dawson's late conduct. "Papa told me something of obligations he was under to Mr. Clarke on Dawson's account, but he did not explain them clearly. I am afraid he may be the means of breaking more hearts than papa's, Ellinor."

And Ellinor, fancying that her sister alluded to herself in the latter part of this speech, coloured deeply as she answered—

"Dawson has been running into debt, I suppose, and obliged to get money to pay his creditors by dishonourable means. But, whatever we may think of his conduct, we had better not exasperate him by reproaches or hard words; for I have reason to believe that he is very reckless—he might be capable of committing some rash act if roused too much."

"Oh, I shall not exasperate him; you need not fear," said Dora, who was determined to have her own way, in spite of Dawson or any one else. "Yet still I cannot help feeling for papa and mamma. Are we to say good-bye to Lady Halesby now?"

"No, I shall write her a note, instead of taking leave of her in person. As to the other people here, I suppose we need not see them at all; they will not mind our going away without bidding them good-bye; at all events, I am not able for it."

" I used to hope Dawson would captivate Lady Mary Shelbank," said Dora, sighing, " for she seemed to like him very much, and you know he is very handsome. And then if he were in difficulties her money would save him and papa; but I suppose if you have quarrelled with Lady Halesby that scheme would come to nothing."

" God forbid that any respectable girl would be led to marry Dawson unless he re-formed !" said Ellinor, earnestly. " Just imagine the fate of any woman married to an unprincipled man, who by the law would be entitled to exercise authority over her and her fortune."

" But every one must take his or her chance in this world, Ellinor. There are a great many unprincipled, cruel men in the world, and yet it is to be supposed that they have either got wives already, or will get them. The law, of course, intended bad men as well as good, foolish men as well as wise, to have authority over their wives and their money. Women must submit to that sort of thing, I suppose, when they have no power to alter the laws of the country. How many men, do you think, would have to remain unmarried if it were a rule that only the wise and good among them were to get wives?"

" A great many, I fear," said Ellinor. " But there is no doubt that, in the old times, when those laws were made, the most foolish men were considered wiser than the wisest women, gifted with higher intellectual and moral qualities. Public opinion has altered upon that point during later years, but the law stands pretty much as it did in the old barbaric times. However, I am sure it will be altered some of these days, when we are mouldering in our graves, perhaps."

"And in the meantime I wish Dawson would prove himself superior to us in moral and intellectual capabilities, and do us some good, instead of keeping us always as poor as church mice, and never caring what becomes of us!" added Dora.

Ellinor then went to write her farewell note to Lady Halesby. She wrote thus:—

"DEAR LADY HALESBY,

"After what has occurred to-day, I think it is better for both you and myself that we should part without again seeing each other. I do not suppose that your feelings towards me can have changed within the last few hours, and therefore I consider that any further meeting would give unnecessary pain to each of us.

"My sister and I are now about to leave Halesby.

"Yours truly,
"ELLINOR BOUVERIE."

It was very hard for Ellinor to have to write "Dear Lady Halesby," and to sign herself "Yours truly;" but, considering that the expressions were merely conventional, and meant nothing more than a form of words, she was reconciled to use them rather than abruptly subscribe herself "Ellinor Bouverie." She dispatched the note to her hostess, and then Dora and she, hearing that the fly from the Halesby Arms had arrived, went downstairs and took leave of the grand old house of Halesby, having seen their trunks and boxes put upon the fly.

It was now quite dark, being past six o'clock of the winter evening, and they met no one but servants on the way downstairs. Fortunately Dora had brought money enough with her to give the domestics liberal donations for herself and Ellinor, and their pride was not wounded in that point. Ellinor was, by far, more bewildered and less able to act energetically than her sister in this emergency; she was quite prostrated for the time, and, seeing her so unusually bereft of presence of mind, Dora exerted herself to the utmost to spare her trouble.

In all that had occurred during that fatal day Ellinor Bouverie had never shed a tear, but she felt stricken down and powerless, as if all her energy of mind and body had left her.

The strife within her heart was dying out, because she had no strength left to keep it up. A sort of numbness was stealing over her now, increasing as she and Dora drove along the dreary long road to Norham, in the bleak February evening.

She had carefully avoided looking at the quaint gate-lodge of the entrance to Halesby, opening on the Norham road, as the fly swept

out of the gate, with its massive ivy-covered
pillars.

Long as the drive to Norham was, Ellinor
was almost sorry when the fly rattled into the
town, passing through the principal street
where the gas was already burning, and the
shops shedding out feeble lights. She dreaded
to go home and have to meet her father, who
had always shown such affection and partiality for his only son, expecting great things
from him; she dreaded to return to the
monotony of her old life of drudgery and
care—now doubly distasteful in prospect, because she would have nothing but bitter
memories to dwell upon. She was conscious
that this heavy chastening of Providence was
not received by her in a proper spirit of submission; she knew her own weakness, and the
knowledge added to her humiliation and her
wretchedness.

Over the quiet, damp road to Evergreen,
the fly passed, and then it stopped at the gate
of the villa, bringing the sisters, at last, up to
the door of their home.

Patty received them gladly, with many expressions of welcome ; but her quick, servant's eye soon detected that neither of the

young ladies were in very high spirits, and
her rejoicing was checked and her voice
lowered in a very few minutes. Probably
she had hoped great things from that visit to
the grand house of Halesby, and probably
she now felt that she had hoped in vain. And
so she sighed, and helped the boxes and bags
down from the fly, and into the hall, and was
half afraid to ask if the ladies would have a
chop or anything nice at tea. Poor servants!
they have often a hard time of it, obliged as
they are to reflect the different phases of their
master's or mistress's conditions of mind. Of
course, neither Captain nor Mrs. Bouverie
had expected their daughters upon that particular evening, and the former felt it was
rather like a presumptuous defying of paren-
tal authority for them to return home in this
sudden way, without having given notice of
their intentions. To be sure Dawson had
done the very same thing about a week before; but then a young man was very different from a couple of girls, who have no right
to independent behaviour. There was something very strange, he thought, in Ellinor
and Dora having presumed to hire a fly from
the Halesby Arms, and drive up to the villa

without previously communicating their intentions to their mother, at least. Then he thought, perhaps, that they had written to their mother on the subject, and that *she* had presumed to defy him and keep him in ignorance of their movements; so that he worked himself up into a most tyrannical temper, and, after quarrelling with the flyman for what he chose to consider an overcharge for the hire of the fly from Halesby, he requested explanations of a most embarrassing kind from Ellinor, respecting her extraordinary return home when no one expected her.

"And where is Dawson?" he asked. " You did not choose, I suppose, to put yourselves under his protection; but drove alone eight miles in the dusk of evening in a public conveyance, hired at an immense expense! . Let me tell you, young ladies, that this spirit of independence won't do at all. When your brother was in the country, you should have waited till he was able and willing to escort you here."

And so this father scolded his grown up daughters, and scolded his wife, whom he blamed for what his grown up daughters had done amiss; and walked up and down the

room, where Patty was gravely laying the
tea things, afraid to make the slightest jingle
of cups or spoons—afraid to tread on the
ground, almost—in fact, afraid her very presence might call down renewed wrath from
that terrible master, walking up and down in
anger.

Now, it is a curious fact that Dora was
scarcely sorry that her father proved himself
so unkind upon that evening. His harshness
to Ellinor and herself made her determine
more than ever that she would endeavour to
escape from a home of misery, and seek the
protection and companionship of some one
whom she could really love and respect.
There was no way to get away from her
home but by marrying, and there was only
one person in the world whom she could bear
to think of uniting her fate with. She felt
thankful that her father did not allude at all
to Mr. Clarke that night. She bore all his
scolding, all his taunting expressions, with
the utmost calmness, because she was thinking altogether of something far more important and far more terrible to her than anything he chose to talk of at that time. It
was poor Ellinor, who had nothing to buoy

her up—nothing but despair before her—
who felt nearly crushed by her father's
cruelty.

Before she went to bed that weary night
Dora sat up and finished, or rather wrote a
completely new letter to her lover in Ireland.
That home scene of scolding and unreasonable anger on her father's part—the discomfort so apparent at Evergreen—everything
combined to make her feel humble and
miserable; and, therefore, she said far more
than she had intended to say to Mr. St.
George when writing to him from Halesby.
She did not care any longer whether she
appeared dignified or not; she wrote the
truth, and that she was not happy at home.
She said her father wished her to marry a
person she did not even like or respect, and
that she was willing to give her hand, with
her heart, regardless of wealth or worldly
prospects. She felt too excited by the events
of the day just gone by to write either very
guardedly or reservedly. Had she kept the
letter for one whole day in her possession, no
doubt she would have altered it, or perhaps
never have sent it to the post-office at all;
but she finished it, directed the envelope most

carefully, and sealed it, having requested her lover very earnestly to let her have an answer without delay.

Next day, when Patty was going to Norham on business, Dora, feeling like a guilty being, gave her the letter to take to the post-office, unseen by any of her family. Notwithstanding her manifold flirtations, this was the first love letter our heroine had ever dispatched to an admirer, and she felt very nervous and perturbed about it. Had there been time to do it, she would have opened it and modified some passages, or altered others —in fact, perhaps, she would have written another letter altogether; but Patty was ruthlessly waiting, basket in hand, ready to go to market, and evidently impatient, and she had to give it to her as it was. Her hand trembled as she put the letter into the servant's grasp, and her heart beat so fast that she was quite faint.

"It is gone now," she said, as she watched Patty going along the road to Norham. "I may expect an answer by Thursday next."

CHAPTER XVIII.

THE LETTER FALLS INTO WRONG HANDS.—
MR. CLARKE TREMBLES.

It was Dora's wish that the letter should be dispatched to Mr. St. George by the mail that left Norham at one o'clock in the afternoon, and consequently she had instructed Patty particularly to go to the post-office without delay ; so Patty made good speed and hastened quickly to the town. But it happened that she had very few minutes to complete her walk in, and when she got near Church Street, where the post-office was, she was obliged to resort to a running pace. While going thus swiftly onwards she met Mr. Clarke, who stopped and spoke to her with that interest which gentlemen in love feel for the serving-people of the ladies they are attached to.

" How are you, Patty?" he asked blandly. " Have the young ladies come home, yet?"

" Oh, yes, sir, they came last night."

" Indeed ! I hope they are quite well ?"

" Yes, sir, very well, thank you," replied
Patty, who was in great trepidation lest she
should be late for the post, yet unwilling
to seem disrespectful to her master's great
friend.

" And has Mr. Dawson Bouverie returned
home also ?"

"No, sir, not yet—only the young ladies.
Please, sir, I am in a great hurry, wanting to
post a letter for Miss Dora; she is anxious
it should go out by the one o'clock mail."

Mr. Clarke took out his watch, and looked
at it.

" Just two minutes to one, Patty," he said,
smiling ; " but if you give the letter to me I
shall see that Miss Dora is not disappointed.

" Oh ! sir, I can run very fast with it,
thank you. There is plenty of time."

" But the postmaster will take a letter from
me after the usual hour of closing the mail-
bag. You need not fear to trust me. I would
not disappoint Miss Dora Bouverie for anything in the world, and she knows that very
well herself," said the barrack-master.

" Yes, sir, to be sure, sir; but if you would

only just let me run on now I would be at the office in one minute."

" But there is always a crowd as this hour about the post office. You will find it very hard to get your letter in, even if you reached the end of the street in time. Give it to me, and I shall go at once with it."

" But you see, sir, she laid her commands on me to post it surely, and I would far rather do it than let anyone else post it."

" Nonsense, Patty ! It must be a very particular letter," said Mr. Clark, with a little scrutiny in his look at the girl's face. " Miss Dora would trust me, you may be certain, faster than some other people. There, now, it has struck one by the church clock. You are too late for this mail."

Patty threw up her hands and eyes in the greatest dismay.

The barrack-master laughed, and stretched forth his hand.

" Come, now, you see there is no other help for it, Patty. I shall save Miss Dora from some dreadful misery about that letter. Give it to me and you will be all right."

" Oh ! if I had only run on at once, sir, I should have been time enough," declared

Patty, whose temper was getting a little soured; but I suppose I mustn't think of posting it myself now. You'll surely get it off, sir?"

And she handed the letter to him.

" I should do far more than that for Miss Dora, Patty," he said, as he took the letter.

His eye glanced at the direction—first at the " Ireland " written at the end of it, then at " Gartoquil Rectory, Donegal," and lastly at " Rodney St. George, Esq., — Light Infantry," and then his face grew rather red, and his brow lowered, but he was not a man who lost his presence of mind very quickly.

" You need not tell Miss Dora Bouverie of this letter being posted after hours," he said, carelessly; " it might annoy her and make her uneasy, Patty, and I should not like her to suffer a moment's anxiety for the world; so just say the letter went off in good time, without mentioning my having anything to do with it; do you hear?"

" Yes, sir. I know the young lady would be very much vexed indeed if she thought I was careless about it," said the girl, who was really concerned, and rather downcast herself.

" Was she very anxious, indeed, about the letter?"

" O dear, yes, sir. I wondered at her, for she could hardly speak; she was out of breath like when she gave it to me, and her face was as pale as paper."

" Humph—indeed! Can you read writing, Patty?"

" Well, not very cleverly, sir," replied the girl, blushing. " I hadn't very good opportunities of learning, being at work since I was quite a child."

" Hum! Well, you may tell your young lady you sent the letter off. Good-day."

And the barrack-master slipped a half-crown into Patty's hand as she hurried away.

Posed and miserable he was, when the girl had left him, standing in the street, with that letter in her hand. *Her* handwriting directing the envelope to the person of all others whom he was most jealous and afraid of in the whole world at present!—the person whom he knew with fear and trembling was at Halesby during the visit of the Misses Bouverie there !

There were very few people or things in the world that could make Allan Clarke

tremble or turn coward, but he trembled now
with great apprehension, and emotion of different kinds, as his eye fixed itself vacantly
on the address of that terrible letter. He
knew very well that young ladies were not in
the habit of corresponding upon indifferent
subjects with young men who were not in any
way related to them. They might flirt with
them, and receive attentions from them in
society, without having any particular meaning in so doing; but writing letters to each
other from a distance is a different affair, and
evinces something more serious than a mere
passing amusement.

Would Dora Bouverie write a letter to Mr.
St. George, and send it all the way to Ireland,
if there had not been a mutual understanding
between them—a regular declaration of attachment on his part, and a regular acceptance of his adddresses on hers?

" False girl that she is!" thought the barrack-master, bitterly. " Yet she will not altogether outwit me: Even still I do not
despair—I will not despair!"

But even as he mentally gave uttterance to
these words, he felt an icy feeling of despair
creeping over him—a despair and a misery

so intense that he had scarcely power to be wrathful or vindictive.

The minute-hand of the church clock close by where he stood slowly but surely glided on its round, and it was nearly a quarter-past one when Allan Clarke had decided to walk down the street in a direction quite opposite to that of the post-office.

All the time that Patty was away at Norham, Dora Bouverie was in a very nervous state of mind, unable to settle to anything, and when the servant came back, she felt half afraid to ask if the letter were posted; but she did ask.

" Well, Patty, did you send my letter off in time ?" she said, trying to speak carelessly.

" Yes, miss, I think it was in time," replied Patty, colouring a little; and then Dora questioned her no more, much to the girl's relief.

Captain Bouverie was scarcely in any better temper all that day than he had been the evening before ; and as Ellinor was out of spirits also, Dora felt the atmosphere of her home most oppressive.

The only thing that gave her any consolation was the fact that Mr. Clarke did not come all that day, nor the next, to call at Evergreen. She was a little surprised at this, but delighted also. Was he going to give her up, and save her the trouble of giving him up? Ardently she hoped it was to be so.

Dawson Bouverie did not return home, or write to any of his family at this time; he left Halesby, of course, the same day that his sisters left it, but he did not go to Evergreen, or inform his relatives there of where he did go to, which scarcely caused them to feel any surprise, as he had often been in the habit of treating them carelessly.

In the meantime, Abraham Barr was nursing his wrath against the barrack-master, who had withdrawn some privileges formerly granted to the upholsterer. No longer were the soldiers employed about the barracks allowed to assist Barr in the removal of furniture from the officers' quarters, or in the arrangement of goods and chattels when they arrived there. The cabinet-maker was obliged to hire men himself, at a considerable expense, to do what he had merely to pay a trifle for before.

No soldier was permitted to lend a helping

hand, as in former days of amity ; and this
proof of Mr. Clarke's vindictiveness roused
Abraham's anger more and more. He could
not lay his mind to any useful work; his
whole aim appeared now to be to search out
whatever might be wrong in the way the
barrack-master discharged the duties of his
office. As ordnance storekeeper, Mr. Clarke
had a great deal in his power as to the patronage of different tradespeople, and rumour
had been afloat a good deal that he had private motives of self-interest in the employ-
ment of some persons who supplied the garrison with necessary articles of consumption.
Envy and malice had, no doubt, something to
do with these reports, but Barr opened his
ears to them, and tried to spy out, with un-
swerving perseverance, everything that could
tend to lessen public confidence in the
barrack-master. Of course this pursuit took
up nearly all his time and thoughts, to the
detriment of more profitable occupation, so
that his family were beginning to suffer
seriously in a pecuniary way. Money for the
daily expenses of the household had to be
taken out of the bank, where it was invested
during past years, and this grieved Mrs. Barr

extremely. She foresaw ruin coming on her-self and her children; and at night she some-times lay awake picturing to her mental vision all sorts of calamities.

Every day there was some fresh cause of vexation between Mr. Clarke and the mis-guided upholsterer, who felt a sort of exul-tation every time the barrack-master displayed malignity towards him, as it kept up his feel-ings of anger and contempt.

Day by day Barr was collecting materials to form a mighty list of accusations against Clarke. His whole soul was absorbed in this exciting task.

* * * * *

When Ellinor Bouverie learnt from her father that her sister had almost given a decided promise to marry Mr. Clarke, she was greatly surprised, as Dora had never hinted a word of such a thing to her ; she was both surprised and a little offended. It seemed so strange of Dora to keep an affair of that sort secret from her. In her own esti-mation, the match appeared a most undesir-able one; she had never liked the barrack-master, and she did not believe that her sister liked him.

"The truth is," said Captain Bouverie, when speaking upon the subject to his elder daughter, "that I owe Clarke a large sum of money, lent to me some time ago to pay some debts of your brother's; and to pay this money back would reduce me to beggary, and not myself only, but all of you.   As it is, I am doubtful whether Evergreen must not be sold to enable us to live.   We could do with a smaller house—a lodging, perhaps—or go abroad and economise there; but Dora would escape much privation by marrying Clarke, and I should not be asked to come down with the money I owe him for a good while—perhaps never."

"And it was Dawson who thus embarrassed you, papa?" said Ellinor, whose sad heart was sinking lower and lower.

Ellinor felt miserable as her father spoke. Dawson seemed destined to bring ruin and disgrace to his nearest relatives.   Only for his misconduct, what a bright fate her own might have been; and, through her, what happiness might have come to her family !   The days were passing, and there was no news from Halesby.

Ellinor dreaded to go to Norham lest she

should meet even one of the servants from
the Park. She had not the slightest expectation that Gerard Lyon would ever seek to see
her on friendly terms again. And now there
was poverty and ruin, and misery of every
kind to look forward to. It was a very bitter
thought.

Morning   after   morning—evening   after
evening—did Dora wait and watch vainly for
an answer to her letter from Mr. St. George.
The first fluttering nervousness of hope and
expectation began at length to give place to
apprehension and serious fears; and finally
she abandoned herself to mortification and
wrathful feelings.

" He knew I would expect an answer
almost by return of post," she thought;
" and he is delaying it on purpose, perhaps,
to try me. If he valued my regard he would
never do this. Perhaps he will be made to
comprehend that I am as unforgiving as I
told him I was."

The more she dwelt upon the frankness of
her letter to him, the more she felt mortifed
and wretched. She feared that she had
written too humbly—too openly. She had
expressed her real feelings with too little re-

serve ; she had relied too much upon his truth and constancy. As the time wore on, bringing no reply from Mr. St. George, she resolved to have revenge—a poor, miserable, short-sighted revenge—such as men and women but too often practice when labouring under similar feelings of mortification. She would sacrifice her own happiness to gratify this revenge, or, at least, to show how lightly she regarded the indifference of her false lover. She would enter into an engagement to marry a person she disliked, to let another person whom she thought had slighted her see that he was nothing to her!

Before her wrath had subsided Mr. Clarke made his appearance at Evergreen, and Captain Bouverie roused himself from his depressed state of spirits to receive him courteously and even gladly. Ellinor was so sad about her father's evident wretchedness that she was almost relieved to see the barrack-master, as it gave him a temporary satisfaction, and when he asked her to go down and help to entertain him she did so, simply from a feeling of pity and affection. It seemed to her as little short of disastrous that Dora should be obliged or induced to marry Mr.

Clarke ; and it confounded her to see her
sister coming in to see the barrack-master
upon the first day he called at Evergreen after
their return from Halesby, with a smile upon
her countenance and a sweet expression of
face, as if she were very happy to meet him.
Even Ellinor was not aware of how much
Dora could deceive and dissemble, but perhaps Mr. Clarke had his doubts of her sincerity. He arose to receive her on her entrance a little coldly at first, and the colder
he seemed the more Dora smiled, and cast be-
witching glances from her blue eyes, while
all the time she was perturbed and miserable,
but powerfully sustained by mortified pride,
and a wish for revenge. Is there any stimulant that gives such courage as anger and a
vexed spirit ?

Allan Clarke looked at her in surprise and
with distrust ; his yellow eyes watched her
with a furtive, scrutinising gaze over and over
again during that visit. He could not believe
her to be really anxious to please him ; he
feared she was even a greater hypocrite than
she was ; but he could not let her off so easily
as she might imagine, he thought ; he would
punish her and her family for her duplicity,

and for the pain she had inflicted on him. He was not a nervous man, and he rarely betrayed emotion, yet he could feel very deeply for himself, if not for others. Nobody could have known what he suffered during that interview with Dora Bouverie and her father and sister, for he was composed and steady of nerve as usual.

Towards the close of the visit, and while standing up to take leave, he asked Dora if she would permit him to speak with her alone for a few minutes; and then Captain Bouverie, who had been looking so haggard and anxious, with his eyes almost wild from intense expectation, that Ellinor's heart was nearly broken, turned quickly to his younger daughter, and said of course she should grant the required interview, and with a cringing, fussy air, not like his usual dignified manner, desired Ellinor to accompany him from the room.

CHAPTER XIX.

THE ANSWER TO THE PROPOSAL.

FOR some days Dora had been aware that her father had been heavily embarrassed, and their home in danger of being parted with ; but these considerations did not influence her in her present resolution. She was cool and determined (or she thought she was), and when Mr. Clarke and she were alone in the room, her heart scarcely beat at all quicker than it had done before. It was some time before she spoke.

"It is now more than the stipulated time for me to learn my fate, Miss Bouverie," he said, anxious to make her uneasy as if he could do nothing more ; "and of course you have made up your mind before this."

"Yes, I have quite made it up," answered Dora, without the slightest hesitation ; "and you may now speak to papa, if you wish. I

am very much flattered at your high opinion
of me, and I hope you may never repent the
choice you have made."

Mr. Clarke was very much astonished at
this reply, so different from what he had expected, but still he felt doubtful.

"And am I to understand, then, that I
have indeed succeeded in winning your affection?" he asked, slowly, as he advanced a
little nearer to her, and stood almost close
beside her.

" I have given you my answer," she said.
" You must know that I intend to accept your
proposal."

" And your whole heart is indeed mine?"

" It is a very poor, worthless heart, I fear,"
she answered, evasively ; " but I will try not
to be very bad, if you will only trust and
bear with me." And she endeavoured to
smile, but the effort was rather unsuccess-
ful ; she felt, too, a little afraid of meeting
the sharp, searching look fixed upon her face,
but withal she was standing her ground
bravely.

" I had fears that you did not intend to
give me a favourable answer," he said, apparently but little elated at her reply. " I

knew how unworthy I was, and I also knew
that there might be a prior attachment on
your part—some one might have won your
love before I spoke to you of mine."

" I do not love anyone else," she said,
firmly, and perhaps bitterly.

" You really never loved anyone else?"
he asked, with the air of an incredulous
inquisitor, rather than that of a very tender
lover.

" Whatever fancy I may have had in past
days can have nothing to do with the pre -
sent," she replied, unflinchingly. " If you
doubt what my feelings now are, you are
perfectly at liberty to withdraw anything you
have said to me."

" Do not blame me for being a little doubtful and mistrustful of my own claims to your
favour. It is my anxiety that makes me
seem, perhaps, impertinent. Heaven knows,
the only strong wish of my heart is to win
your love. I can scarcely believe it possible,
after spending so many hopeless days of late,
that such happiness is really in store for me."

" Then you do not think it possible for me
to be your wife?"

" Scarcely : it is almost too much to believe,

after my late despairing thoughts. You know
yourself whether I had any ground for these
fears—you can say whether they were utterly
without foundation. But it was my firm
conviction that I had a rival of a very for-
midable description."

" I am not going to enter into any particulars of the past, or of what might or might
not have been my feelings then. I told you
I should give you a decided answer respecting your proposal after some time of consideration, and I give it to you now, to receive it in whatever spirit you may think
best," she said, looking him full in the face,
and speaking with as much coolness as if she
were offering him some article of merchan-
dise which she was rather indifferent about
his purchasing.

" And I am to believe that your heart is
indeed mine—that I have had no such rival
as I dreaded—that you are not accepting my
proposal merely out of pique, or anger with
anyone else ?"

" I cannot answer any more questions of
that sort; you must be satisfied with the
reply you have already received. If you
wish to give me up pray say so at once."

And, rising from her seat, Dora walked away
to a window recess, and stood looking out
on the garden, feeling very strangely.

Very beautiful she looked, with the pale
winter sun glancing on her shining hair and
on her face, so delicately fair, with just a
slight trace of pain and sad thoughtfulness on
the lightly-pencilled brow—a trace of what
she had suffered for the last ten days of suspense and mortification.

Mr. Clarke walked towards her, after
watching her with undecided feelings for a
few minutes. Should he hold her at her
word, and accept the answer she had given
him, in spite of his better judgment? Or
should he let her off, and try to forget her—
try to believe that he had never loved her,
and did not love her now, notwithstanding
what he suspected, and what he knew? Did
not vanity come whispering to him even then,
and flattering him that she might yet return
his affection, and be won over by all his love
and care?

He stood beside her once again, but she
still kept looking out at the garden.

" I have not offended you, I trust ?" he
said, speaking more gently than before.

"Oh, no. Of course you are at liberty to think and act as you consider fit," she answered. " If you doubt me I cannot help it, and if, doubting me, you choose to withdraw anything you have said, perhaps it would be the best course to pursue for your happiness. I told you long ago that I was not a person likely to make any home very happy. I have not been a particularly amiable daughter or sister, and I do not expect to make a very good wife."

" But you said you would try to become changed under the influence of a new sphere of existence—for the sake of the person who would have no one else to look to for comfort and affection ?"

" I did not say exactly that ; I said I should try not to be very bad, if you would trust me. You do not know, perhaps, how unforgiving and angry I can be when slighted or thwarted. Even to myself I am pitiless at such times ; but if I am trusted and borne with, and not provoked by injustice or misunderstanding, I can act a tolerably amiable part."

" You need not fear that *I* shall ever provoke your anger by unkindness," said her companion, now assuming the humility of the

Q 3

lover. "I should not dare to treat you with indifference, much less with injustice. You have been too long the one bright star of my life to become ever an object to be regarded carelessly by me. You will be to me always the one being on earth for whom I shall entertain the same feelings of ardent love and attachment. Heaven knows what I have suffered for you during the last year! Ay, for the last year, for you had been in my thoughts long before I dared to breathe a word of my love to your father or yourself. My love for you during many months has been of the most intense description, and you must excuse me, dearest, if it has led me into any unreasonable observations. You must forgive me for anything I may have said or done, because I have been nearly frantic through endeavouring to maintain an air of calmness, and often of indifference, when my heart was bursting with agony and disappointment!"

Dora was moved a good deal by her lover's passionate declarations, but not very tenderly. His earnestness and his warmth were unpleasant to her—far more so than his cold questioning and doubtful manner had been.

Was it too late to draw back now, and remain a free woman, unfettered by the most hateful bonds? A free woman she might be, but never more a happy one, she thought, under any circumstances, humbled and heart-stricken as she felt; and, besides that, she had her revenge to complete—her indifference to show to the person who had slighted and mortified her. Was she not now perfectly convinced of the reason which that contemptible person had for quitting Halesby, and the whole neighbourhood of Norham, in such an unexpected, sudden manner? Did she not know that it was to cast her off, and cause his faithless protestations of love to come to nothing? He had repented of all he had said to her; he had probably begun to think that she was not of as high a family as he was himself, and that wealth was necessary to his happiness. Altogether there had been something most mean and inexcusable in his conduct; and she must let him see that his unprincipled behaviour could make but little impression upon her. When he should return to Norham—if ever he could return—he should find her the wife of another man. She only wished that that other man had been of higher rank and

greater influence in the world than he was,
that her revenge might be the sweeter, and
the self-love and vanity of her false lover
wounded the more acutely. But that other
man was the only person just at present
offering her his hand, and giving her thus
an opportunity of speedy retaliation. Her
revenge, to be complete and striking, must be
immediate.

And these were her thoughts as she stood
beside the man whose wife she was purpos-
ing to become—whose eager eyes were fixed
upon her face with a look of intense admiration—whose arm was encircling her slight
figure with all the confidence of a favoured
suitor.

"And so, my beloved one, we understand
each other now?" he said, looking tenderly
into her eyes, which had lost much of the
sweet, coaxing expression she had thrown
into them upon her first appearance in the
room, and were now a little dull and vacant
looking.

"I suppose we do," she replied, stifling a
very heavy sigh that was struggling for an
outlet. "You have not repented of your
proposal?"

" Repented !   No, but I am beside myself
with happiness, my own dearest one !" and,
clasping her to his breast, he impressed a
passionate kiss upon her lips.

END OF VOL. II.

T. C. NEWBY, 30, Welbeck Street, Cavendish Square, London.